Seduction Most Wicked

Jen Bradlee

SEDUCTION MOST WICKED

Copyright © 2022 Kirsten S. Blacketer/Jen Bradlee.

This is a work of fiction. Similarities to real people, places, or
events are entirely coincidental.

Printed in the United States of America.
First Printing, 2022
ISBN: 978-1966905158

Cover Art by The Midnight Muse
Written by Jen Bradlee
Published by BlackShip Press
Kirsten.blacketer@gmail.com
https://kirstensblacketer.com/jen-bradlee/

Dedication

For all the ladies who love villains.

A Letter from the Author

Dear Reader,

Welcome and thank you for selecting *Seduction Most Wicked* for your reading pleasure. I truly hope you enjoy the story and fall in love with the characters.

Allow me to preface with a warning. If you're not a fan of anti-heroes with dominating and questionable morals, explicit intimate scenes, or graphic language and violence, then this may not be the book for you. For a complete list of content forewarnings, please visit kirstensblacketer.com/jen-bradlee.

If that's exactly what you're looking for, then allow me to welcome you and proceed. Thank you for choosing The Prince of Whispers as your literary companion.

Sending warm regards and best wishes your way. Remember to be kind and love one another.

Sincerely,

Jen Bradlee

Table of Contents

Year 1442 A.D.
SCOTLAND
Northern Hold
IRELAND
ENGLAND
Balmont Holding
Marian's Cottage
Monastery
Culver
MERADIN
WALES
KEY
Capital
Landmark
Village
Port

Chapter One

Was Crispin dead?

The concern for her husband's life weighed as heavily upon her as the bounty once had. Ruby wrested herself from those distracting thoughts, determined to focus on the task before her. The harvest festival would take place within a fortnight and much of the planning remained. There was no time to worry about something over which she had no control. She wandered among the tables in the great hall, her gaze skimming over the selections brought for her approval by the villagers to decorate the town.

Two moons passed since her marriage and the coronation, and still, she could not find comfort in her new position. While she knew her life as queen would not be as exciting as her life as an outlaw, it granted her small windows of opportunity to place her mark upon her kingdom without being branded a traitor. She longed for the freedom of the forest, but the path that lay before her bound her both to Crispin and the people of Meradin. This truth proved unshakable.

"Have you made a decision, your majesty?" The servant girl, Ivy, stepped forward. Her hands folded demurely in her lap, eyes downcast.

"I have not." Ruby waved her hand across the selections. "I am indecisive. They are all beautiful in their own way. Perhaps you could offer some perspective, Ivy."

Ivy's gaze snapped up to meet hers. "You wish for my opinion?"

Ruby regarded her with a smile. "Aye, I trusted your judgment when it came to my trousseau, why would I not grant you the same leave when it comes to decorating for the harvest festival?"

"I am your humble servant, my queen. Truly." Ivy hesitated when the door opened behind her and Vivienne entered the room. "I do not wish to overstep the bounds of propriety."

"How in heaven would you selecting some garland be overstepping?" Ruby inclined her head to Vivienne who came to a stop beside her.

"I agree." Vivienne brushed her fingers over the woven garland. "Which would you choose, Ivy?"

"This greenery would stand out the best against the individual stands with the red and gold accents. These garlands would be best around the inner and outer bailey." Ivy itemized each piece placing it perfectly in the mind's eye. When she finished, she bowed her head.

Ruby motioned to the other servants. "Take these with instructions for the villagers to have more made for the celebration." The weight on her shoulders lightened with the decision. She turned to Ivy. "My thanks for your help. I am confident in your selection."

"As you wish, your majesty." Ivy bowed and followed the other servants out of the room bearing an armful of garlands and fabrics.

Once the solid doors closed leaving her alone with Vivienne, Ruby collapsed on a nearby bench. Longing and exhaustion clawed at her chest. She gazed at the vaulted ceiling wishing it were canopied expanses of blue sky.

"Come, my dear." Vivienne ventured toward the staircase leading into the heart of the castle.

Ruby pulled herself to her feet wondering where Crispin's mother intended to take her. They wove through the corridors and passed Crispin's chambers. Her heart ached. She missed him desperately.

The day after the wedding, Henry's family disappeared from the capital of Culver without taking their leave. They gave no indication as to the reason for their sudden departure. Even though Ruby felt nothing but relief at their absence, Crispin and Henry immediately banded together in his private chambers only to emerge and leave the castle the next morn, abandoning the tournament which was to be held in honor of their marriage. He kissed her thoroughly before leaving without a word of explanation.

After two moons passed, the only assurances of his safety she received were from the messenger relaying information to the privy council. Part of her resented him for departing with such haste and shrouding his intentions in secrecy.

Vivienne stepped through the archway leading to Crispin's personal garden. The flowers faded on the vine, retreating from the burgeoning chill of the approaching winter. Ruby brushed her fingers over the bruised petals.

"Come, let us tarry a while." Vivienne sat on the stone bench against the wall and gestured for Ruby to join her. "Speak to me, child. I cannot offer comfort if you do not unburden your heart."

"My apologies." Ruby settled onto the bench and leaned against the wall.

"I do not want your apologies, I desire to know what thoughts plague you." Her soft voice held no censure, only concern.

"I cannot help but wonder if I have made a mistake." She toyed with the gilded hem of her gown. "I made a much better outlaw than I do a queen."

"You judge yourself quite harshly." Vivienne took her hand.

"'Tis the truth. I may be of royal blood, but deep in my breast beats the heart of an outcast." Ruby attempted to collect the chaos of her thoughts into coherent reasoning. "I cannot even make the simplest of decisions in preparation for the festival, how am I going to influence the kingdom?"

"You are adrift in an unfamiliar sea. I understand." She nodded with sage understanding. "Even though I was raised in the court from birth, I had not been the first choice. With three elder sisters, my parents placed low expectations on my marriage ever forging a strong political alliance."

Ruby studied her profile as she spoke. Everyone knew Queen Vivienne was the Bavarian cousin of Catherine of Valois.

But these intimate details of her past were not something often discussed among courtiers. Vivienne knew better than to foster any gossip of the royal courts.

"The first time I saw Edgar, I wanted to strangle him. He paid me no mind, focusing all his attention on my elder sister, Sophia. They were engaged within a fortnight." Vivienne chuckled at the memory. "Before they were to leave my parents' estate and return to Meradin for the wedding, Sophia eloped with the stable master's son. My father offered me as a replacement for Edgar's stolen bride."

"Against your will?" Ruby bit back the fury of indignation on her mother-in-law's behalf.

"Not completely against my will." Vivienne winked with a grin on her lips. "I seized it for the opportunity it was. A chance to become queen and exert some influence, even if it came through my husband. Although, I found myself floundering the first few years. Nothing prepared me for the reality of wearing the crown."

Her story tugged at Ruby's heart. "So there is hope for me?"

Vivienne drew her close and pressed a kiss to her head. "Aye, my child. There is hope for you still. Do not be disheartened. I shall instruct you, should you need it, but trust your intuition. It will not lead you astray."

"How can you be so certain?" Doubt fluttered in the pit of her stomach even though the words bolstered her confidence.

"When you were in the forest living as an outlaw, which did you rely on more, your training or your intuition?"

Ruby pondered the question for a long moment, but the answer formed in her mind immediately.

"You saw my son in trouble and acted on intuition alone, relying on your training to come naturally."

"Aye." The reasoning behind her assessment soothed the chaos in her mind.

"Even with all the training in the world, it means nothing if you do not trust your intuition. It will guide you to the right path, as it always has before." Vivienne's gracious smile warmed her.

"My thanks for your words of wisdom." The restless unease

in Ruby's soul settled leaving just a smidgen of lingering doubt deep in the pit of her stomach.

"I have faith in you, my dear. One day, you will be the regaled as the most beloved queen in all Meradin's history."

Ruby snorted at the statement but covered her mouth quickly. "My apologies. I did not mean to laugh."

"You will see. One day." Vivienne stood and brushed her hands over her fine crimson velvet skirt. "I have some things to attend. Perhaps you should take some time to rest in your chambers, you look pale. Have you been eating?"

"Aye. I have not slept well since Crispin departed." Inside, relief washed over her. She was exhausted but did not wish to retreat from her duties. "A rest will do me wonders."

"I understand. I shall send Ivy with some warm broth." She paused in the doorway and glanced back at Ruby. "And do not fret, my dear, Crispin will return soon. Lord knows you will need your strength for when he returns."

Ruby's face warmed at the implication of her words. After their wedding night, the entire castle witnessed the ferocity of Crispin's desire for his bride. The thought of his return left her body warm and planted a desperate ache deep inside her.

Once she reached her chambers, she freed the pins from her hair and loosened the plait before lying on the coverlet. Images of her husband floated through the haze of her memories. His wicked mouth on her skin. His teasing fingers parting her folds. His body fitting perfectly to hers. Ruby's breathing came in shallow bursts as the restless ache consumed her.

A knock at the door pulled her from her sensual thoughts.

"My queen." Ivy entered the room bearing a tray. "My apologies, I did not realize you were abed."

"'Tis no matter." Disappointment replaced the aching need. She rose from the bed and settled in the comfortable chair beside the hearth.

Ivy placed the tray on the table beside her. "Will you require anything more, your majesty?"

"Nay, I shall be quite content." She lifted the bowl to her

lips and sipped the broth. Her stomach twisted and lurched against the scent, making her flinch.

"My queen." Ivy knelt beside her upon observing her distress. "Are you well?"

"'Tis nothing more than a passing pain." She pressed her hand against her midsection and groaned. "The taste does not bother me, but the aroma leaves me ill. Perhaps I should have some peppermint tea."

The maid studied her for a long moment, her sharp gaze narrowing. "I shall fetch it now."

Ruby nodded, bracing her head in her hands. The door closed behind Ivy leaving her alone with her thoughts once more. She attempted a few more sips of the broth, but the scent became more unbearable. With a groan, she pushed it away and returned to the bed.

Lying down seemed to soothe the persistent discomfort, but removing the scent eased the churning in her abdomen even more so. Ruby rubbed her hand over her stomach. A tendril of fear crept into the back of her mind.

When Ivy returned, she urged Ruby to sit up in bed and made her comfortable by propping cushions around her before providing the steaming mug of tea. The pungent mint immediately soothed her. It brought memories of her childhood with Marian and Guy to the surface. A tendril of homesickness wove around her heart constricting it. How she missed them. Perhaps she should send for Marian to come visit. She possessed ways to ease her concerns when all others failed.

"My queen, I hope this is not forward of me, but I am concerned for your health." Ivy met her gaze directly. "Shall I send for a healer? Or perhaps the Queen Mother?"

Ruby sipped the tea. "I appreciate your concern, Ivy. But I do not wish to cause anyone undue worry on my account. I am perfectly well."

Ivy fidgeted with the hem of her kirtle but her gaze remained steady. "Ma'am, 'tis possible you are with child."

Hearing the words aloud voiced the fear she refused to acknowledge. Ruby pinched her eyes closed and conceded. "Aye.

'Tis a strong possibility."

"Such news should be cause for celebration, should it not?" Ivy asked, her green eyes bright. "The king will be overjoyed at the news of an heir. The whole kingdom will celebrate!"

Ruby grasped Ivy's hand and held it tight. Fear pulsed through her, threatening to tear her in two. "Promise me you will tell no one. Not a soul. Not until…well, until I am certain."

Ivy took her hands between her own, her expression softening. "I promise, my queen." A frown pulled at her mouth. "But you must at least inform the Queen Mother. She will understand your plight."

"I will think on it." Ruby swallowed hard not allowing herself to consider the implications of the conversation with Vivienne. "I do not wish to give her false hope."

"A child is a blessing." Ivy smiled, and her face transformed, revealing a hidden beauty.

"Aye." Ruby took another sip of her tea. How had such a lovely maid escaped the notice of every man in the castle? The passing thought made her pause, but she pushed it away.

A child would be a blessing if only she could be certain of who the father was. Even though she had been faithful to Crispin, one night created chaos and conflict in her mind. Her body warmed at the memory of being blindfolded. The touch of two men. The pleasure they wrought with little effort. And the shame that stalked her every day since.

She hung her head. Could it be possible this child belongs not to the king but to his closest friend and confidant? The thought alone left her filled with a writhing agony. What if the truth somehow emerged? Was it not treason to betray the king? To tarnish the monarchy with this blatant infidelity. Would Crispin consider such a revelation treason?

"All will be well." Ivy took the cup from her hands and set it on the bedside table. "You will see. The king will return soon and all will be well."

"I do hope so." Ruby settled back against the cushions and closed her eyes.

"If you require anything, I shall be in the kitchens." Ivy

retrieved the tray with the bowl of uneaten broth.

"Grammercy, Ivy. You have been a gift from heaven during the king's absence."

"I live to serve you, my queen." Ivy bowed and left the room.

"What am I to do?" Ruby whispered against the coverlet, clutching the fabric tight. The sound dissolved in the empty room. "I cannot tell Crispin. I cannot tell Vivienne. Where else can I turn?"

Panic consumed her in waves. Slowly it pulled her down into the darkness of her deepest fears. If this child were not truly the heir of Meradin, what horrors would Crispin unleash upon her? Even though the events of that night were of his ministrations, his command, would he still blame her for fostering a bastard in her womb? She buried her face against the cushions.

Unable to quell the rising panic, Ruby rose from the bed and darted into the hallway. With determined steps, she wandered the corridors until she located Mina, her young maid, outside the king's presence chamber.

"Fetch the swordsmith's apprentice, Matthew. Have him meet me in my chambers. Quickly." Ruby kept her voice low.

With a nod, Mina darted down the hallway and around the corner.

Ruby returned to her chamber and paced the floor near the window overlooking the inner bailey. The autumn wind rattled the thick pane of glass. Her hand settled on the curve of her stomach. Truth be told, whoever the father of this child, she would treasure it regardless. She would defend and protect it until her dying day.

A knock at the door shook her from her thoughts, and she bid them enter.

"You summoned me, your majesty?" Matthew bowed low. His young face smeared with dust and dirt. His rough hands twisted his cap.

"Aye, Matthew. I require you to travel to my mother's cottage and bring her to the castle post haste." A calm settled in the depths of her soul as she issued the directive.

"At once, ma'am." Matthew bowed once more and retreated from the room.

Ruby detested using the young man as her own personal messenger, but she trusted no one more than she did the young blacksmith. She came to the aid of his family on multiple occasions and gave him a position within the castle to ensure his family a comfortable life. In response, they swore fealty to her. A fact she chose not to exploit. However, in her desperation, she required someone who could be trusted completely and knew where to find Marian.

Until she spoke to her mother, she would remain in her chamber. Vivienne would certainly be understanding and supportive if she chose to trust her with this revelation, but she required the comfort and advice of a woman who knew the depths of her soul like no one else.

Marian would know what path to take. How to best reveal the news to Crispin and the kingdom. But this conversation would entail revealing the sinful details of the night of passion spent with both Henry and her husband. Could she face the shame of revealing such information to her mother?

She bit her lip. Perhaps she had been hasty in summoning Marian, but it was too late. She would need to reveal the truth sooner or later. If anyone could understand without passing judgment, it would be her mother.

After retrieving her now cold tea, she settled before the hearth and stared into the flames. The moments drifted away until the sun set beyond the window and darkness filled her chamber. When Ivy arrived with some bread and dried fruit, she nibbled on the fare and found it fortified her without making her ill.

Before she drifted off to sleep, Matthew arrived breathless at her door. "I did as you commanded, my queen. But the cottage was empty."

Disappointment gripped her heart but it also gave way to relief. "My thanks, Matthew. Please find something to eat in the kitchens before returning to the smithy."

"Many thanks, ma'am." His youthful grin infected her with hope.

Once Matthew took his leave, Ruby prepared for bed. On the morrow, she would visit her mother. Crispin was not present to dictate the boundaries of her royal prison and determine whether she could leave the castle grounds. She would take two guards and make the journey without incident.

For the first time in weeks, a sense of peace settled over her. Perhaps she merely needed to escape the confines of these stone walls. Ruby could not run forever, but she could embrace the opportunity to forget for a while.

Comforted by her plan, Ruby nestled beneath the blankets. Soon Crispin would return, turning her whole world upside down once more. While she longed for his return and the comfort of his touch, his presence hung like a shadow over the castle.

In truth, they were still so little acquainted and newlywed. There was still much to learn from and about one another. But one thing she knew for certain. She would never be able to keep a secret from the King of Meradin. Especially not one with such monumental consequences.

Chapter Two

After traveling across the country for nigh on two months, Crispin arrived at a solid conclusion. There were most certainly traitors in their midst. When Henry's family vacated the castle the day after his marriage and coronation, it solidified his suspicions about their involvement in something more nefarious than mere treason. He had hoped to confront them about their involvement in the raid set to kill his bride years ago, until they disappeared into the night without an explanation.

Henry urged his horse into a trot, bringing his blood bay gelding alongside Crispin's dappled gray. "We should arrive at the castle by late afternoon, sire."

The soldiers both ahead and behind them lay far enough to ensure their conversation remained somewhat private. Crispin shifted in the saddle, glancing over his shoulder to be certain his words would not be overheard.

"When we arrive, nothing of our journey will be discussed until I have taken the opportunity to speak with my bride. Is that understood?"

"Aye." The firm set of Henry's jaw belied his irritation.

"Once I speak with her, we will convene with the privy council to address the information our journey uncovered."

"And what, pray tell, would that be precisely?" Henry rounded on Crispin. "'Tis my impression we uncovered nothing of value and are left with more questions than answers."

Crispin smirked. "'Tis more an observation of what we did not find than what we did."

Henry's attention shifted to the small cluster of knights riding ahead. His silence spoke adequately enough for Crispin to place the direction of his thoughts.

"I do not hold you responsible for the treasonous actions

of your family." His voice carried low between them. "However, they will be punished for their part in past actions."

"My father and brothers have not the mind nor the inclination to betray the crown. They acted solely out of greed. The idea was placed in their minds by someone with power and influence. Mind you, I am not standing in defense of their actions. They should be held accountable for their role in the raid." Henry shifted uneasily in his saddle. "There is more to this than we are privy. I sense there may be trouble brewing on the horizon, sire."

"I am of the same mind." Crispin allowed his gaze to roam through the trees along the road. During the extent of their journey, he anticipated an ambush of some kind or at the very least a confrontation. Yet at every estate, every village, they were welcomed with grace and warmth, extending congratulations on his marriage and bestowing felicitations of health and prosperity.

When they reached Henry's familial estate, they found it vacant. In Crispin's mind, this solidified their guilt. Over the following weeks, they visited every holding of his vassal lords, making inquiries and forming bonds that should be maintained to ensure the kingdom's safety from outside influence. Their input merely confirmed his assertion that the baron and his sons were in league with someone to bring chaos to the kingdom of Meradin. 'Twas treason for certain, but more lay beneath the muddied surface if they could only clear the waters.

"Why do you wish to speak with the queen before you address the council?" Henry's question broke through his thoughts.

"As the Lady of the Forest, she spent much of her time among the peasantry. She possesses information about the brigands and thieves who roam through these forests. Perhaps she knows of someone who could lead us to uncovering the hole in which your family has crawled." His grip tightened on the reins. When he found them out, they would wish he had run them through while their bellies were full of his fine wine. Death would be too good for them. They would talk, and then they would pay the price for treason in flesh.

"You expect her to betray her fellow outlaws?" Henry chuckled at his assumption. "Her loyalty runs deeper than most."

"Still, 'tis the last possible path before I put a bounty on your family's head." He held Henry's gaze. "Once I reveal their involvement, it will tarnish your reputation, no matter what I decree to be the truth."

Henry squared his shoulders. "I am prepared for their censure. It matters not. My life is in service of the king and to protect the people of Meradin. My family has no loyalty to the crown or the kingdom. They chose their path, therefore let them reap the consequences of their decisions."

"Even if it casts your character into doubt?" Crispin studied his companion's reaction carefully. In all their years together, never had he seen Henry as committed to his conscience as in this moment.

"Aye. Put the price on their heads. Bring them before the council and let them suffer their fate." Henry turned his stoic gaze toward the road. "Had you arrested them at the wedding feast, we would not have to chase their shadows across the country."

Crispin glowered at the observation. "Would you have me ruin my wedding and coronation? Cast it into infamy with the arrest of my High Steward's family for crimes against the crown and treason?" He tutted. "My bride deserved to have the memory of such a momentous day free from the horrors of her past."

"My apologies, sire." Henry shook his head and pulled the flagon from the saddle to take a drink. "I only wish to avenge the wrongs done to my queen at the hands of my family."

With a nod, Crispin accepted the flagon. "Aye. 'Tis a noble pursuit." He drank heartily of the spring water they gathered that morning. "I had not anticipated the cowards would flee before the morning light."

"We will uncover their location and reveal the depths of this plot before it can bring more harm to the kingdom and the queen." Henry's statement sounded much like a vow.

"What of your king?" Crispin teased him.

Henry bowed half-heartedly in the saddle. "I mean no offense, sire, but after all these years, I should not have to prove my loyalty to you. If our past exploits do not speak for themselves, then nothing I say now will quell your demand for fealty."

"'Tis the honest truth." Crispin allowed himself a laugh. "When we were young, I often wondered why you chose to spar against me rather than Simon or Francis." It was the first time he mentioned the name without bracing for the impending judgment of being compared to his saintly elder brother.

Henry's bark of laughter echoed through the trees. His horse danced beneath him, tossing his head in irritation at the noise. "Francis always held back when we sparred. And Simon, well, he always waited for the moment of weakness to strike. For him it was not about learning, it was about domination." He lost himself in the memories. "None of the other knights in training came close to providing a challenge."

"Then why choose me?" The question pulled at his conscience. He could almost see the day they formed their unbreakable bond, clear as a painting in his mind.

"We were the same. Two younger sons desperate to prove ourselves." Henry shrugged his shoulder as though the confession did not matter.

It struck the soft flesh of Crispin's soul and twisted. A tenderness poured forth, one Crispin had not anticipated. Even though they both had brothers of flesh and bone, they chose to form a bond even stronger than family.

"But 'tis more than likely I chose you because you overcompensate when you fight, allowing your aggression to cloud your judgment." Henry laughed. "'Twas quite simple to bait you with a taunt or a jab. Made the fight unpredictable. I learned more from battling you than I learned from the best knight-at-arms."

Whatever tenderness he discovered for Henry dissipated at those words. "Perhaps I should put a price on your head as well."

Henry sobered, his grin transforming into a scowl. "For answering your question honestly?"

"Nay, for admitting your king's faults." He relished the look of pure dismay on his companion's face.

"My apologies, sire. I meant no disrespect." Henry steeled his jaw. "But you have faults aplenty. No man is without fault. Not even your brother, God rest his soul."

At the mention of Francis, his heart hardened. Since childhood, he made no effort to hide his disdain for his elder brother. The perfect prince. The bastion of honor and chivalry. The legend of his brother's heroic actions and sainted generosity rang throughout the land. The country mourned his death just as his parents had.

All the while, Crispin sat quietly while he secretly celebrated his brother's demise. 'Twas nothing personal. He loved his brother, although he loathed the expectations placed upon him by Francis's angelic shadow. Once he was dead, Crispin was free, and moreover, he was the heir.

"Francis was no saint." Crispin clenched his teeth, the words hissing at the strain he placed upon them. "But he was a good man." The thought of his brother being king and possessing Ruby near drove him to frenzied madness. He shook his head. "God rest his soul."

The ease of their banter shifted into a tense silence almost as if the ghost of Francis reached from beyond the grave to tarnish his victory. Crispin's mood darkened with every passing league. The sun began its descent over the horizon, casting long shadows across the road.

They passed through several small villages and wove around Skye Lake. When they reached the king's road leading into Culver, Crispin's spirits lifted. Even Henry noticed the improvement and began to sing a ditty.

"Oh where the stone is cold and lonely, there I shall find my lady fair." Henry carried a tune better than the bard who frequented the castle.

"Methinks you are in hope of finding a willing wench to warm your bed this eve." Crispin teased him.

"Aye." Henry's easy smile faded. "What of you, sire? Are you not anxious to see your bride?"

The world faded around him as he envisioned his Ruby stripped bare and sprawled across his bed. Her body flushed with need. Lips parted and begging. Unbidden, his cock pressed insistently against the constraints of his clothing. Any longer in the saddle while burdened with this state and he would go mad. He shifted and pushed the vision of his erotic beauty aside.

"What think you?" He tugged at the leather covering his cock.

Henry laughed. "At least you can be certain of the pleasure awaiting you."

"Aye." Crispin spied the castle through the trees ahead. He wished to urge his horse into a gallop and finish the distance in half the time, yet, he refrained. The king spurred on by the thought of his queen would never instill respect and authority. He smoothed his hand over Ghost's shoulder and gave the horse a gentle pat.

When they finally arrived at the gates, darkness surrounded the castle. Torchlight flickered across the stone as they entered the inner bailey.

The pages rushed forward to gather their horses and a small crowd gathered around them. Crispin's gaze skimmed the bailey for Ruby's warm smile. But after a few moments, dread settled in his gut. Where in the devil was she?

Ignoring the crowd and Henry's questioning gaze, he rushed into the dining hall and wove through the corridors, searching every room on the path to her chamber. When he reached the door of her personal chamber, he opened it without pretense.

A fire warmed the room, but inside he found only her young lass and a buxom, handsome maid he did not recognize. "Where is the queen?"

Both the girl and the woman dipped into a low bow.

"The queen has gone for a ride, sire." The woman dared to meet his gaze. "She has not returned yet."

"Gone for a ride?" Fury pulsed through his body. "God's blood, teeth, and bones." He slammed the door and stormed down the hall.

He would find his bride. Then punish her for not remaining where she would be safe until his return. Heaven help him, she would learn to heed his commands or suffer the consequences.

Chapter Three

At dawn, Ruby slid from the warm embrace of her bed. Her restless sleep did nothing to soothe the gnawing worry in the pit of her stomach. She needed to speak to her mother, if not to gain some comfort then perhaps to receive guidance on what path she should take.

She dressed in her leather trews and tunic, donning a doublet and her boots last. Traveling this way would ensure no one cast her a second glance. No one would expect the queen to venture from the safety of the castle dressed as a man and without a bastion of guards.

As she retrieved her wool cloak from the wardrobe, a soft knock at the door set her heart racing. She draped the cloak over the back of the chair as the door swung open.

Vivienne stepped into the room, her knowing gaze skimming over Ruby's clothes without a hint of judgment. "Venturing out of the castle?"

"Aye. I wish to visit my mother. She was not home yestereve when I summoned her." Ruby fidgeted with the belt around her waist.

"Might we speak before you take your leave?" Vivienne gestured to the chairs beside the fire which was now little more than embers leaving a chill in the room.

Ruby took the seat opposite and fought against the panic clawing at her chest. Crispin's mother settled gracefully into the seat. She wore a blue gown with gold trimming. Her dark hair tucked into a coiled net. Vivienne reflected the true image of a regal and refined queen. Ruby's inadequacies rose to the surface when she compared herself to the poised woman beside her.

"Did my words not offer you any comfort?" Vivienne's gaze softened with kindness. "I understand I cannot offer the same understanding as your mother. The bond you share with her is as rare as it is strong. But I do wish to foster the same trust between us if you will allow me."

"You are too kind. I did take comfort in your words of wisdom." Ruby tried to smile, but her worry outweighed her ability to lie.

"Are you concerned about the child?" Vivienne's question pierced her soul.

"How did you know?" Ruby gaped, her hands covering her midsection protectively.

"A mother's intuition." Vivienne waved her hand. "But also, when your courses come, the maids know. There is always talk amongst the servants, even the most loyal and discreet."

Ruby hung her head. "When Crispin returns, I will have no choice but to inform him, lest he hears it from the servants or his council."

"I have instructed them to keep the matter silent for the moment." Vivienne took her hand and gave it a comforting squeeze. "But when he returns, you must tell him without delay."

Uncertainty bubbled up inside her making her stomach churn. She shook her head, unable to put a voice to the words for fear of judgment. *Harlot. Traitor.*

"Do you have reservations?" Vivienne's voice soothed her, but the fear remained. She stroked the back of her hand gently.

Ruby nodded. Her response strangled in her throat.

"As to the father of the child?" Vivienne pressed further. The question echoed in her mind like a crack of thunder in the darkness.

"How did you know?" Her eyes filled with tears.

"As I stated before, there is nothing sacred within these walls. Every action is known to the servants and gossip travels through them like the river into the sea." Vivienne stated the fact as though evident. "My son often acts rashly out of hedonistic desires. I have already chastised him for using both you and Henry in such a manner. Perhaps this will be the realization he needs to see the error of his ways."

"You knew of that night?" Ruby hid her face behind her

hand.

"I learned quickly to become the silent observer within these walls."

"Why did you not confront me sooner?" Ruby asked, finally able to face her companion.

"In time, I believed you would come to me. But when I noticed the signs of your change, I knew I could no longer prolong the inevitable." Vivienne folded her hands together. "I am your ally. We are bound by a common thread. My son and your husband. 'Tis our duty to serve the king."

"Serving his wishes is exactly how I found myself in this position." Ruby exhaled sharply, dashing the tears from her cheeks. "When he discovers I am with child, will he not question the validity of his heir?"

"'Tis possible. However, revealing it will expose you and Henry to criticism. I doubt he would sever the ties of the two he holds closest to him." Vivienne pondered the possibilities for a moment. "Nay, my son may be rash and self-indulgent, but he is also calculating and possessive."

"Are you of the mind he already considered this possibility?" Ruby pondered the implications of such a motive. But why would he manipulate her if she were already bound to him?

"I love my son, but he is no saint." Vivienne twisted the ring on her finger. "When he was a child, he would constantly compete with his brother, as well as the other knights in training. Where Francis always followed the code of chivalry, Crispin would plot and scheme, finding ways to subvert and twist the situation to suit his needs. In many ways, Crispin outperformed his brother, but it did not make him a good leader. He cares only for himself.

"Francis sacrificed himself to save innocent lives trapped by a fire, while Crispin stood by and watched." A tear slid down her cheek. "I cannot be upset at either for their actions. Had Crispin acted as Francis, I would have lost both my sons that night."

"Such a decision could not have been easy for either of them," Ruby added softly. "In such a moment, is there a proper path to take? Or is it merely God's will manifested?"

"I would give my life to see my sweet Francis again." Vivienne cupped Ruby's cheek, her gaze tender and loving. "But you would never have been happy with him. Crispin is as much your destiny as you are his. No matter what comes, know this. You are his treasure and he will do whatever is necessary to protect you."

She closed her eyes, soaking up the warmth of Vivienne's touch and her words. "I know."

"When he returns, tell him. The longer you wait, the more unpredictable his reaction will be."

"Aye." Ruby dropped her hands into her lap and took a steadying breath.

"Are you still set on visiting Marian?" Vivienne rose to her feet.

"I am." Ruby studied her profile as Crispin's mother strode toward the door.

"Very well." Vivienne paused in the doorway. "I shall have your escort prepared. Do not fret, I shall adequately disguise them. No one shall know the queen has taken to her forests again." Her understanding smile set Ruby's concerns to rest.

"I shall be down momentarily."

"Meet me at the postern gate." Vivienne nodded and closed the door behind her.

Alone and resolved in her determination, Ruby plaited her hair and pinned it beneath a net, hiding the bound auburn tresses beneath a dark hood. She retrieved her cloak and slung her leather satchel across her chest before making her way through the castle down to the inner bailey.

Four horses stood beside the postern gate. Three guards dressed in simple garb were already mounted and waiting. Vivienne appeared from behind her mare, Ginger, and held out a wrapped parcel.

"A gift for your mother. Send her my best wishes and tell her my offer still stands."

"I will." Ruby acknowledged the message. Even though she wished to inquire further, it would take most of the day to make the journey and return. The days grew shorter and conversation would burn through whatever precious daylight remained. "My thanks, mother." She embraced Vivienne, who welcomed the gesture willingly.

"Travel safely and return swiftly. Crispin could return any day, and if he arrives while you are absent, there will be blood." Vivienne's warning echoed in her mind as she mounted her horse.

The guards followed her out the gate. The moment she broke free of the castle walls, her heart soared. This was where she belonged. Among the people tangled in the dark forest, bent low over her mount at a canter toward the king's road.

Liberty embraced her, alleviating the chaos from her mind and setting her heart soaring above the treetops like a falcon on the hunt. With a glance over her shoulder to ensure the guards followed, she pushed Ginger harder, savoring the pounding of the horse's hooves on the dirt and the wind rushing around her nearly pulling the hood from her head.

Near midday, they approached the monastery where she frequently delivered medicines. Perhaps she should stop and allow the horses a moment to rest. It would do her good to see Brother James again. Her mother's cottage was not far. They could spare a few moments to rest and refresh themselves.

Ruby pulled Ginger to a halt outside the monastery's gate. A small cart sat parked beside the stone wall. Near the tree line, a mule grazed on the tall grass.

She dismounted and tossed her reins to one of the guards. Before she could knock, the door swung open, revealing the scarred monk.

"Brother James, I trust you are in good health." Ruby's mood bolstered at the appearance of her friend.

"What a joyous surprise." Brother James stepped aside and invited her inside the garden, leaving the guards to watch the horses. "This is truly a blessed day."

"Ruby?" The warm, familiar voice washed over her like a soothing balm.

"Mother?" Ruby spun around to find Marian with a basket

on her arm full of herbs and flowers.

The basket tumbled to the ground and the women rushed together to embrace. Brother James stood to the side, silently watching their reunion.

"I was on my way to visit you." Ruby laughed. "I sent Matthew to fetch you yestereve, but the cottage was empty."

"Aye. You know I always spend this time of year gathering what remains of the herbs and roots I need before winter." Marian shook her head. "It seems you have forgotten."

"Well then, let us celebrate this day. I shall have some refreshments prepared." Brother James clasped his hands together.

"That sounds delightful. And also, some libations for my guards outside, if you please."

"As my queen commands." Brother James bowed humbly and took his leave, allowing Marian and Ruby time to speak alone.

Marian slipped her arm around Ruby's shoulders and led her to a small bench tucked along the stone wall. "What news could warrant the queen to stray from the comfort and safety of her castle?"

"I am with child." Ruby's confession spilled from her lips like water bursting free of a dam.

With a squeal of joy, Marian wrapped her arms around her, pulling her into a warm, comforting embrace. Ruby sank into the loving gesture and savored it. 'Twas not often she indulged in such shows of affection since she had become queen. When finally granted such simple contact, Ruby relished it, realizing how much she regretted its loss.

"My gem, I have prayed for this day." Marian drew back and cradled Ruby's face in her calloused hands.

Ruby covered her mother's hands with her own, guilt burrowing into her conscience. "As of this moment, only yourself and two other souls are privy to this knowledge."

Marian arched a brow in question. Her gaze narrowed and a frown stole her delight. "Why have you no cause for celebration of such joyous news?"

Ruby took a fortifying breath and explained the events casting their shadow over her joy, forming doubts in her mind. She chose the minutest of details in which to tell her tale, unable to bear the judgment and embarrassment of such a scandalous situation. As she drew to the end of her story, the marked lines on her mother's lovely face deepened with the force of her concentration.

After a long, thoughtful pause, Marian took her hand. "My precious gem. What is done, is done. There is no changing the past. It is now part of your life story. Allow it to make you stronger, wiser, and more discerning in the future, but never allow it to define you."

The heavy ache around her heart eased at her mother's comforting words. Emotion choked her. She squeezed her hand in response, unable to form the words to show her gratitude.

"Will you tell the king when he returns?" Marian asked, her voice low. Her gaze skimmed the garden searching for signs of Brother James's return.

The uncertainty and fear coiled once more in the pit of her stomach. "I have little choice in the matter. If he discovers the truth from anyone but myself, it will only infuriate him."

"Do you fear his wrath?" At Ruby's shrug, Marian brushed a lock of hair beneath the hood and tipped her chin up forcing their gazes to meet. "The king is many things. While he can be cruel and manipulative, 'tis obvious he cares for you beyond anything in this world. Do not underestimate his adoration or his possessive nature, but in the same manner, be observant of these actions for he reveals his true feelings hidden deep within them."

Ruby pressed her cheek into her mother's palm and pressed a soft kiss to her sun toughened skin. "You truly are wise, mother. I pray one day I have half of your wisdom."

Marian chuckled. "There were many hard-learned lessons through my life to earn me such knowledge. Time and experience are harsh taskmasters, but they serve us well if we choose to heed their instruction."

"I thank you for your honest council, mother. Truly, you have set my mind at ease." Ruby drew her mother into her embrace once more and held tight. She missed her dearly. These last few months spent learning of her past and adapting to her new life left her adrift and lonely.

She missed her life as the Lady of the Forest, but even more than that, the freedoms she once took for granted. Life as an outlaw was far more forgiving than life at court. While the common folk of Meradin loved and praised their new queen, many of the courtiers paid her little courtesy, seeing her as an impostor of sorts.

Brother James reappeared with several other monks who bore cups full of mead made with honey from the monastery's small apiary. They delivered the beverages to the guards outside the wall and enjoyed an afternoon spent in the last remaining days of autumn gathering herbs and roots for Marian to use in her herbal remedies.

As the sun began to drop on the horizon, Ruby helped her mother pack the items in her small cart. The mule and cart had been a gift from Crispin, Marian told her. A method for her to deliver her goods to those who needed them. Although he never mentioned the thoughtful gift, Ruby understood it was his way of repaying Marian for her role in Ruby's upbringing.

This small measure of freedom, escaping the keep for even a long afternoon, left her refreshed and revitalized.

"I thank you for your hospitality, Brother James." Ruby gifted him a small bag of coin. "Please send word if there is anything I can do for the monastery. Your work is important to those in the nearby villages."

"Your majesty is generous and gracious." He bowed low. "I am your humble servant, my queen."

His words were sincere, but Ruby disliked the distance they created between them. Once their banter had been easy and comforting, and now they left her with a cold emptiness. She shook off the unease and turned to her mother who hung a lantern on her cart to lead her home in the darkness.

"Vivienne says her invitation still stands," Ruby murmured as she gave her mother the parcel.

"I cannot abandon my home and take up residence in the

castle." Marian tutted and place it with the herbs. "I will visit soon. You have my word." She climbed into the cart and clicked to her mule. They ambled down the path in the opposite direction of the castle.

"Your majesty, we should return." The guard handed her Ginger's reins.

"Aye." She hoisted herself into the saddle and spun Ginger around.

Brother James stood in the archway, his face shrouded in shadow beneath his hood. He offered a lantern, lifting it high. The light brought his scarred visage into relief. She nudged Ginger closer and took the lantern.

"May God go with you." He bowed once more and retreated into the garden, closing the door behind him.

A chill of dread trailed its fingers along her neck. Ruby pulled her cloak tighter around her shoulders and urged Ginger into a trot away from the monastery. The three guards followed behind, their lanterns bobbing in the darkness illuminating the path. They wove through the forest until they met the king's road.

Ahead in the distance, a light rose up. It swayed and grew brighter. There must be another traveler along the road. One of the guards rode ahead to meet with them. Curiosity tugged at her, but she remained safely tucked between the remaining guards.

A rider broke free of the travelers ahead and raced toward them. Ruby drew Ginger to a halt, allowing the two remaining guards to step between her and the oncoming rider.

The thundering of the horses' hooves on the dirt road matched the pounding of her heart. She rested her hand on her dagger, wishing she had brought her bow.

The oncoming horse reared when the two guards with swords drawn stood between them.

"Stand aside by the command of your king," a voice boomed through the darkness. The lantern light glinted off the gold hilt of his sword.

"Crispin." Ruby pushed Ginger forward. The guards fell

back, giving them wide berth.

In one swift movement, Crispin swung down from the saddle and pulled her from her horse. His mouth crashed over hers in a bruising kiss, stealing her breath. She clung to him and thread her fingers in his hair. His grip tightened and he growled.

"You have returned." The statement slipped free between kisses.

"Aye." He slid his hand along her thigh, drawing a moan from her lips. "I returned to find my bride has disobeyed me." The flickering light danced in his eyes. "And I intend to punish her accordingly."

Ruby clutched his doublet tight. "I told you before, husband. I am not a possession to be locked away in a tower. If I wish to visit my mother, I shall do so."

Crispin steeled his jaw and climbed back into his saddle. He pulled Ruby up across his lap.

One of the guards took Ginger by the reins and led her behind him. Ruby stared back at him until Crispin's whispered words reached her ear.

"Have care, sweeting. You may be the queen of Meradin. But you are mine in every conceivable way, and I will claim you, body and soul, until you are weak and begging for release."

Ruby's heart pounded and her body responded to his sinful whisper. She clung to him in silence, both apprehensive and aroused by his wicked promises. For all the days to venture outside the castle, she chose the day of her husband's long-awaited return to break the one rule he put in place for her protection.

He would punish her that much was certain. The question remained…how?

Chapter Four

Crispin's cock ached from the persistent press of Ruby's backside. While he did not regret the decision to ride back to the castle with her in his lap, it took a saint's restraint to keep from pulling her into the darkened forest and taking her against the tree in full view of God and kingdom. He held her tight with one arm clasped around her waist. The other held the reins loosely against Ghost's withers.

Henry and the guards took the lead upon the return to the keep. This gave Crispin the ability to speak with Ruby without fear of being interrupted.

God's teeth, he missed her. The scent of her skin stoked the fire in his loins as effectively as the sway of the horse beneath them. The motion created delicious friction, bringing their hips into a familiar rhythm. His grip on her waist tightened.

Ruby leaned her weight against him, softening with every step closer to the castle. She removed her hood at his command, baring the long column of her throat.

"Why did you not summon your mother to the castle?" He murmured the question against her skin.

"I attempted to do so, but desperation propelled me to seek her out myself."

Crispin raked his teeth across the sensitive expanse below her ear. "What drives you to such desperation that you would risk my displeasure by leaving the keep?"

Ruby shifted beneath his touch, but he did not miss her soft moan. "Do not tease me, my liege. I am in no mood for your seduction."

He wrapped his hand around her throat. "And I am in no mood for your games." He growled, irritation slowly edging out his body's insistent demands for release. "The guard tells me you met with your mother at a monastery just over the ridge."

"Aye. We often trade with the monks for items from their gardens to make tinctures and salves." She gasped when he dropped his hand to cup her breast through the doublet. "She was gathering the last herbs before winter comes."

"And you knew to find her at the monastery?" He squeezed, wishing there was nothing separating his hand from her warm flesh.

"Nay. We stopped only to rest the horses for a moment, and Brother James led me to the gardens where I found my mother gathering herbs." She arched back against him and licked her lips.

"Who is this monk that you trust him so easily?" Crispin found trust nearly impossible. He abhorred the thought of someone having such unfettered access to his most prized possession.

"He is a good man. Honest and caring. I have known him several summers." She turned enough to study his face. "He is a man of God dedicated to the service of those in need. No harm would come to me in his presence."

Crispin scoffed. "You are far too trusting."

She turned away. "And you are far too cynical."

"I have seen the dark depths of humanity. Given enough incentive, even the most God-fearing man will sell what remains of his soul if it grants him his heart's desire." Crispin shifted his hand to her hip and flexed his fingers inside his gloves.

"Have you sold your soul, my king?" Ruby's question pierced the darkness surrounding them.

"Aye." Crispin gritted his teeth and urged the horse into a canter. He held her tight as they wove around the guards.

Henry glanced at them but said nothing.

The king's road lay open before them, flooded with moonlight guiding their way. Crispin's arm tightened around Ruby. They moved in tandem as Ghost quickened his pace. In the distance, the towers of the castle rose above the treetops.

After days of traveling, he wanted to collapse in his bed and bury his cock inside his wife, yet he found himself riding through the darkness, searching for his wayward bride. A culmination of fury and rage and relief wound tight inside of him threatening to erupt.

How could he have forgotten the stubbornness she wielded so efficiently? Even after this time apart, she did not soften. Ruby challenged him. For a brief moment, he thought she would bend in supplication, and yet she stood proudly against his demands, driving her heels into the dirt like a beautiful, stubborn mythical creature. Placing a crown on her head did nothing to calm her wild nature. In truth, it encouraged her dissent.

Crispin gently slowed Ghost's pace when the village came into view. He allowed the beast to breathe easy. Ruby's body stiffened when he drew her back against him.

"When you fight against my wishes, sweeting, you will find yourself even more tightly ensnared," he murmured against her ear.

He barely noticed the decorations hanging from the cottages and shops in the village. His sights lay solely on the tall, fortified gates straight ahead. As they approached, he called out to the guards, demanding entry.

They moved quickly to open the portcullis and allow him into the outer bailey. By the time they reached the inner bailey, the quiet yard filled with the bustle of servants coming to offer their aid.

One of the stable boys took Ghost's reins. Crispin slid from the saddle and helped Ruby to the ground. She pulled from his touch and glared at him. Without a word, she pushed through the servants and darted into the keep.

Crispin fought the urge to chase her. The thought alone made him hard as steel. He wanted to capture her in the hall and bend her over the great table. He wanted her screams of pleasure to echo off the vaulted ceilings. He clenched his hands into fists.

Instead of feeding the beast raging inside his breast, he took a breath and gave instructions to the servants.

His gaze roamed the bailey. Even in his absence, his mother had maintained order. Ruby would be a wonderful queen in time, but she knew nothing of keeping a household of this size functioning efficiently.

Henry and the guards entered the bailey. He crossed to where his friend dismounted.

"I expected you to be distracted with your bride." Henry grinned.

"Aye. Once she retracts her talons, I will tend her." Crispin's gaze narrowed at the door where Ruby disappeared into the castle. "The monastery where they rested. Do you know of it?"

"I have never spoken to the monks there, but I have passed it on several occasions." Henry handed the reins to a page. "Why do you ask?"

"Ruby spoke of a monk who lives there." Crispin rubbed his jaw. "On the morrow, take a few sacks of grain and deliver them to the monastery. I wish to know more of this monk. Brother James."

"Is this jealousy over her conversation with a man of God?" Henry chuckled.

"There is none pious enough to turn away from a temptation as rare as my Ruby." He sneered. "No man is a saint, remember?"

"Aye." Henry swept into a bow. "As my king commands, it shall be done."

Crispin gave a curt nod of approval. "I am not to be disturbed for the remainder of the night."

A sparkle of knowing lit Henry's eyes. "Of course, sire."

Assured his men had things in hand, Crispin retreated into the keep. The familiar scent and warmth infused him. *Home.* He wove the path to his chamber and found his servants waiting. With brief instructions to prepare a bath, he abandoned his chamber to seek out his wife.

Outside Ruby's chamber, he paused in an attempt to calm the need racing through him like a raging river. He knocked on the door and waited.

"Leave me." Her voice echoed through the wood.

Crispin ground his teeth and pushed the door open. "I warned you, sweeting. Nothing can keep me from taking my pleasure in your bed."

Ruby jumped up from where she sat near the fire and pulled her dagger from the sheath. The special weapon he had specifically designed for her as a gift on their wedding day. The jeweled hilt glinted in the firelight.

"You intend to wound me?" Crispin slowly pulled at the strings lacing his doublet.

"If I must." She tipped her chin up. The long tunic she wore pulled low, baring her shoulder. Her hair flowed like a copper river over creamy skin. His mouth watered at the sight of her luscious curves and tight nipples outlined by the thin fabric.

"Would you deny a starving man a feast?" He pulled the doublet free and dropped it to the floor.

Her eyes flashed with fire and heat. She backed away, keeping the tip of the dagger aimed at his heart.

Crispin dropped his hands to his hips and cocked his head. "Come now, sweeting. If you truly wished to bring me harm, you would have done so when we rode together." He softened his voice. It would be easy to simply disarm her and take what he wanted, but he relished the challenge of seduction. "These sleepless nights spent apart from you have left me aching. Tell me you have not felt the same loss."

The dagger wavered in her hand. She licked her lips. "Aye. Loss has been my companion these past months. You locked me away, forbidding I indulge in things that bring me pleasure."

"You are no longer the Lady of the Forest, notorious outlaw. As the Queen of Meradin, priorities triumph personal pleasure." Agitated, Crispin pulled his belt free and teased the leather between his fingertips.

Ruby lowered her weapon. "Has the king foregone all personal pleasure since taking the crown?"

"In all things but you, my treasure." He crossed the gap between them and wrapped his hand around her arm. Instead of tightening his grip, he smoothed his thumb down over the inside of her wrist. The dagger fell to the floor with a clatter.

Crispin pressed a tender kiss to the sensitive skin beneath her fingers. Her eyes fluttered closed at the gesture. With ease he gathered her into his embrace, she melted against him, her hands clinging to his tunic.

"The thought of you drove me to madness. I longed for you every moment." He threaded his fingers in her unbound hair and cradled the back of her head. "Long nights spent awake with no way to slake the hunger. I cannot count the times I took myself in hand at the thought of being buried inside your warm cunt."

Her cheeks pinkened and he savored his ability to make her blush with mere words. He wanted to see her body bloom with such vibrant color as he brought her pleasure.

Unable to restrain himself any longer, Crispin claimed her mouth. She opened for him, matching his fervor with equal need. Ruby tasted sweeter than he remembered. Her scent infiltrated his reason, drawing him into a dark haze of desire. He held her tighter, molding her curves to his body.

She fisted her hands in his hair and plundered his mouth. He gathered handfuls of her tunic and tugged until it gathered at her waist.

Ruby broke the kiss to remove it completely. She stood bare before him. His hungry gaze skimmed down over her curves reigniting the inferno of lust simmering inside him. Her fingertips trailed between her breasts and over the soft swell of her stomach.

Crispin fought the urge to toss her on the bed and bury his head between her thighs. He swept her into his arms and carried her out of her chamber.

"Where are you taking me?" she squealed, fighting to free herself from his hold.

"To my chamber." He stalked down the hall and kicked open the door.

The two servants who stood next to the steaming tub of water quickly bowed and scurried out of the room. They closed the door behind them.

Ruby wiggled until he set her on the foot of his bed. She tossed her hair back and glared at him. "Overbearing brute."

Crispin shrugged and shed what remained of his clothing. He smoothed his hand over his hard cock. Her gaze followed the motion, making her jaw snap shut. With a grin, he stepped into the water and sank into the scalding heat. Once he settled, he offered his hand.

"Come, join me."

With an obvious sigh, Ruby stood and sauntered across the room, swaying her hips. His cock reacted with a jerk. She stepped into the tub, giving him a glimpse of the wet folds between her thighs before sinking into the water.

Crispin pulled her against him, splashing water out of the tub and onto the floor. Her back settled against his chest. His cock nestled against the cleft of her ass. He grasped her breasts in his hands and let their weight rest in his palms. Her breath quickened as he brushed his thumbs idly over her hard nipples.

"Tell me of your journey." Her request broke through the haze of his lust.

"There is not much to tell." He indulged her curiosity, teasing her with his fingertips while he spoke. "Henry and I traveled to his family's holding, but they had not returned."

"Perhaps they fled to the continent?" Ruby tensed beneath his touch. Whether from the conversation or his ministrations, he could not tell.

"Perhaps." Crispin trailed his fingers down over her stomach. She parted her thighs and lay her head back against his shoulder. "We traveled to every holding in the country. I questioned every member of my court. They know nothing of Balmont's treason."

Ruby moaned at the first slide of his fingertips against her cunt. He reveled in his ability to bring her pleasure with a simple touch. Parting her folds, he explored her, gently teasing until her moans turned to panting gasps. She bucked her hips against his hand.

Crispin released her and retrieved the jar of soap. Her body slumped against him.

She spun around. Her glare cut sharper than the dagger she wielded earlier. Without a word, she attempted to stand. He rested his hand on the nape of her neck.

"Patience, sweeting." He kissed her hard and the soap

dropped to the floor forgotten.

She grasped his cock in her hand. His moan echoed off the walls. Her touch set him aflame. Bucking his hips, he met her gaze boldly and grit his teeth, fighting the rush of pleasure.

Ruby stroked him. "All is fair in seduction."

Crispin gripped the edge of the tub as she quickened her pace. He battled against the rising release. Two months without her and one simple touch had him close to spending.

He enclosed her wrist with his hand, ceasing her torment. Her eyes blazed with equal parts defiance and confidence.

"Aye." He rose from the tub, pulled her from the bath, and dragged her to the bed where he bent her over the coverlet.

Ruby wriggled against his hold, but he held her fast. She shifted to glare at him over her shoulder. Her wild hair covered half her face. Her lips parted at the press of his cock at her entrance. He teased her, sliding over her wet folds before driving into her with a single thrust.

A strangled cry ripped from her throat, but her body welcomed him easily. Her heat gripped him tighter than her fist had. He moved, savoring the sweet mewls of pleasure she made. With every stroke, her moans grew louder, filling the room. He gripped her hips in his hands, driving harder and deeper needing to wring every drop of ecstasy from her.

Her fists gripped the coverlet, and she buried her face against it to smother the sound of her wanton cries. Crispin slid his hand beneath her and urged her pleasure higher with the gentle stroke of his fingertips. He would not last. Her cunt squeezed him tighter.

When she reached the pinnacle of her pleasure, her body clenched around him. 'Twas all the encouragement he needed. He came hard, spilling deep inside her.

He pressed soft kisses along her shoulder and down her back. She trembled beneath him. When he pulled away, a wicked satisfaction filled him at the sight of his seed staining her thighs.

Crispin pulled her into his arms and brushed her hair from her face. Sated, she met his gaze, but he glimpsed the fire banked deep in the depths of her bewitching eyes. He kissed her again, slowly this time drawing out the moment.

"Take the bath." He gestured to the tub. "I want you clean so I can taste your sweet cunt before I take you again."

"Methinks you enjoy treating me like your personal whore." Ruby broke from his hold and stepped into the tub.

"Darling." He tutted with a shake of his head. "You are no whore. But you are mine and I will take what is mine until we are both sated into a stupor."

She took the soap and washed quickly. Crispin admired her as she did so, lounging in the chair beside the fire with his cock in hand.

Even though he wanted her again, he was not blind enough to miss the barrier she erected around her heart. Something happened while he was away, but he knew the only way to uncover it would be to coax it from her lips. Fortunately, seduction was his greatest strength.

"Are you well, sweeting?"

"Aye." Her smile did not fool him. The light did not quite meet her eyes.

Her response solidified his observation. Something was amiss with his Ruby, and he would uncover it. Perhaps it had something to do with her visit to the monastery.

Henry would return with answers, then he could ask her directly.

This night he would make her forget all but him and drown them both in blissful abandon until dawn.

Chapter Five

Henry Balmont regarded himself as a patient, honorable, and loyal servant to the King of Meradin. However, more time spent in his king's company would drive him to drastic measures, like regicide.

A night spent in the comfort of his own bed gave him the rest he truly required after such an arduous journey. He took no joy in investigating the treasonous activities of his own family. Since he abandoned their care to take up residence in Culver as a knight in training, the bonds that once tied him fast to his kin became frayed and untethered. Crispin was more his family than his own brothers. Still, he craved solitude after traveling in close quarters for such a length of time.

He rose with the sun, hoping to make the journey both to and from the monastery before midday. The dawn light broke through the small window in his chamber. He dressed in a simple tunic and hose, forgoing any markings of status or heraldry. His mind drifted to the revelations garnered from their impromptu tour of the kingdom.

At first, the news of his family's involvement in the raid meant to kill Ruby seemed outlandish and cruel. Over time, the pieces of the mystery slowly painted a vivid picture of their underhanded skullduggery. Their absence upon his and Crispin's visit to their land in the north left him with no illusions. They bore the guilt as plainly as if they signed a written confession to their bloody deeds.

Henry took meticulous notes during their journey, tracking to whom they spoke and their responses to the king's inquiry. It seemed as though only his family bore the signs of treason in the whole of the kingdom. His mission remained to protect the royal family, at all costs, even at a great personal loss to himself.

Before the wedding, nigh on two months in Crispin's constant company would have been a welcome distraction. Since Ruby's appearance, Crispin's personality, while still brimming with charisma and calculating indifference, shifted toward focusing on his responsibilities. This should have been a positive attribute, yet Henry found his company insufferable, especially in the absence of Ruby's companionship.

Love, it seemed, possessed the power to transform even the most stubborn of men. At the core of his being, Crispin was still the same self-indulgent, hedonistic man, however, Ruby's presence in his life slowly chipped away at the stone wall surrounding his friend's heart. He hoped the siege continued, knowing she would win in the end if only she persisted with the determination he observed on several occasions.

After pulling on his boots, Henry fastened his belt, securing his sword on his hip. He slipped from his chamber and ventured to the kitchens. With a few sweet words of compliment, cook packed him a small satchel of assorted foods to enjoy during his journey.

Henry stepped out into the bailey with a bounce in his step. His gaze skimmed the servants milling about the grounds preparing for the upcoming festival as well as performing their daily duties.

At the sight of a worn maid's cap, his heart leaped. Could it be Ivy? The maid disappeared into a small crowd. By the time he reached them, she had vanished. Disappointment crushed his hope. Since their passionate night together, Ivy became a distant, aching memory. He longed to see her again. Perhaps she left Culver after their encounter. It mattered not. She did not carry the same affinity for him.

He pushed aside the desire to search the keep and ascertain for himself whether or not his mind played tricks on him. Crispin tasked him with visiting the monastery and interrogating the monk. While his conscience warned him of the king's obvious jealousy being the prime motivation for this endeavor, Henry seized it as the perfect opportunity to escape the confines of his position, if only for a short while.

The young page presented the reins to his blood bay gelding. He pulled himself into the saddle, and the horse danced beneath him sensing his restlessness. Henry reined the horse around and urged him toward the gate.

Once he exited the village, he urged the horse into a canter. The king's road led them north deeper into the forest toward Skye Lake. He found the well-marked fork in the road and took the less traveled branch leading toward the monastery.

The road narrowed, becoming rougher. He slowed his pace to a walk and munched on his treats from the kitchens. Finally, in the distance, the distinct aged stone of the monastery rose into view through the trees.

He pulled his gelding to a halt outside the modest keep. The monastery lay several leagues from the village inn near the lake where they lost Francis in the fire. Henry pushed the painful memory deep into the recesses of his mind.

The large wooden doors loomed in the shadows. He knocked twice, the sound echoing in the corridors inside. After several moments, a monk opened the doors, his hood tipped back revealing a squat, balding man.

"May God grant you mercy, traveler." He smiled with warmth and welcome.

"My thanks, brother." Henry pulled off his cap. "I am searching for Brother James."

"Ah yes, you will find him in the gardens. Come." The monk turned and led him down the passageway. They wove through the corridors, stopping at a worn wooden door. "Through here."

"Grammercy." Henry bowed his head and stepped through the doorway into a deceptively large garden tucked inside the stone walls.

He walked along the pathway until he found a figure hunched over a freshly turned bed of dirt. "Brother James?" Henry asked, approaching cautiously so as not to intrude unannounced.

The monk turned, his face hidden in the shadows of the hood. "Aye."

Henry tucked his cap into his belt. "I come on behalf of the king."

"The king." Slowly the monk rose to his feet, brushing the dirt from his robes as he straightened. "What business does the king have with a humble servant of God?"

Henry stepped back in surprise. The monk's height rivaled his own. His broad shoulders squared beneath the plain brown woolen robes. The hood concealed his features, but his words came clearly, although rasped and deep, clearly unnatural.

"You met with the queen yestereve, did you not?" Henry cleared his throat and came directly to the point.

"Aye. She sought a moment's refuge during her travels." He tucked his hands deeper into his robes.

"You knew her prior to this encounter?" Henry studied the hooded monk, wishing he had a clearer view of his profile.

The monk turned away. "Her mother provides medicines for the afflicted who seek our care. She often utilizes the herbs from our garden in her concoctions. We have been acquainted for several years."

"What are your intentions toward the queen?"

"I have no designs but God's." The monk's response echoed behind him as he wandered down the path in the opposite direction.

"And yet the queen seeks out your council," Henry snapped, but the monk ignored him.

Furious at the impertinence of the man, Henry reached out and grasped him by the arm. He spun the man around to face him, knocking the hood back.

Henry recoiled at the sight of the puckered flesh stretched tight over much of his face. The scarring was beyond anything he ever encountered. It wove intricate patterns from his throat, across his face, consuming much of his head. What hell had this man endured to reach this state? Even his scalp lay bare and crisscrossed with thick, marred flesh. His blue eyes flashed with irritation before a passive calm overtook them.

The monk frowned. "Does my appearance shock you?"

"I…" Henry cleared his throat unable to find the words to

express his surprise and regret. "Please forgive me."

"'Tis of no consequence. I have grown accustomed to the stares, but I still choose to hide my visage as it causes many discomfort." Brother James lifted his hands to replace the hood, but Henry held up his hand.

"Do not feel compelled to hide on my account." He narrowed his gaze, studying the man's profile as he faced him fully. A small swath of untouched skin on his left side made Henry pause. A nagging familiarity tugged at his conscience. "How did you…"

"Receive the scars?" Brother James finished the question. He sighed heavily and pulled the gloves from his hands. They too bore the same puckered scars. "A fire."

Fear gripped Henry's heart in an ironclad fist. "What fire?"

The monk's gaze burned brilliant blue. "An inn near the lake. I attempted to save those trapped in the inferno, but I was the only survivor."

"Francis." The name slid from Henry's tongue unbidden. Even though he had no proof of the monk's tale, the more he studied the man before him, the more it confirmed his suspicions.

"I have not gone by that name for many years." Francis clasped his hands before him. His voice calm and clear.

"How the hell did you survive?" Henry asked astounded by the revelation. "Why have you not come home? You allowed us to believe you dead for years." Anger and betrayal replaced disbelief. He surged forward and grabbed Francis's robes. "We mourned you!"

"I could not return. Surely you understand. Look at me." Francis rested his hands on Henry's until he released his hold. "God has blessed me, and I am thankful for his provision."

Henry stepped back and raked his hand through his hair. A slow realization hit him with the force of a sword blow knocking him into the tree beside the path. "Crispin. When he discovers the truth…" The words lodged in his throat, choking him. "He will be furious."

"Crispin is the king. I have no intention of challenging his claim to the throne." The monk's voice remained calm which only served to agitate Henry further.

"But he is not the rightful King of Meradin." Henry pointed to Francis. "You are."

"I am no longer that man, Henry."

"You must return to Culver with me." Henry paused, his eyes widened at the implication of such a revelation. "Does Ruby know your true identity?"

"No one knows." Francis cocked his head. "Except for you."

"God's blood, teeth, and bones! I cannot shoulder this knowledge in secret." He raked his hand through his hair, exasperated at the thought of hiding this from Crispin. "I cannot. I will not. You must return with me and reveal the truth to Crispin…to your mother." His heart clenched at the thought of Vivienne's reaction to uncovering the truth of the son she thought she buried so long ago.

Francis's gaze narrowed before dropping to the ground. He closed his eyes and inhaled deeply.

"Your mother deserves to know her son yet lives," Henry added with conviction.

"And what of my brother?" Francis voiced the question burning with uncertainty in the back of Henry's mind.

"It does not matter." Henry gestured wildly.

"It does," the monk replied softly. "And if I refuse?"

"Then I shall send the royal guard to escort you to Culver where you will stand before the king and reveal your past as well as your intentions." Henry straightened to his full height and squared his shoulders bracing for a fight. "Either way, you will return to face your family as well as your fate."

A long tense moment passed between them. Henry rested his hand on the hilt of his sword. Finally, Francis released a heavy breath.

"As you wish." He returned his hands to the pockets of his robes. "Allow me to fetch my cloak and relay my departure to my brothers."

Francis opened the door from the garden leading into the

monastery. He led Henry back to the main door where he left his horse tethered and then closed the door behind him.

While he waited, Henry pondered the implications of this joyous but unexpected news. Crispin would be furious. He paced the small path while the possibilities conjured like wisps of smoke in his mind. No matter how they approached this revelation, there would be fury and bloodshed.

Francis appeared around the side of the building riding a donkey.

Henry stared with his mouth open at seeing the man he once knew to be the bravest, most powerful knight in the kingdom dressed in rags and riding an ass.

"Shall we?" Francis asked, maneuvering the donkey around Henry.

Without hesitation, Henry mounted his gelding and followed Francis. At this pace, they would not return to the castle until dark. Until then, he had time to think and plan his own funeral, because Crispin would certainly kill him for returning with Francis.

They traveled until the sun dipped low over the horizon. Francis provided little conversation, instead, he requested tales of home. Henry obliged him even though he desired more details about the fire and his subsequent survival. Francis assured him he would relay the tale in due time.

As they approached the castle, Henry led them to the postern gate where the soldiers allowed them entry without a thousand eyes observing their presence. Torchlight flickered over the bailey as he handed the reins to the page who eyed the hooded monk curiously.

"Where is the king?" Henry asked the boy.

"In the hall, supping with the queen." The boy led the animals to the stables, leaving Henry alone with Francis.

"Come." Henry led the way, weaving through the corridors and up the servant's stairs until they reached the king's private garden. "Wait here."

This would surely end poorly. He made his way to Vivienne's chamber and knocked, hoping she would be in her room and not at the evening meal with Crispin and Ruby.

The door opened revealing a young maid.

"Where is the Queen Mother?" he asked, glancing over his shoulder searching the barren hall plagued with shadows.

"Who is it?" The door opened wider revealing Vivienne wearing a regal gown of deep red and gold. Her eyes widened at the sight of him. "Henry. What brings you here?"

"Please, come with me, your majesty." He bowed in an effort to hide his trepidation.

"Has something happened?" She nodded to her maid and followed him down the hallway.

"There is a guest in the king's garden. He wishes to speak with you in private." Henry led her swiftly to the quiet gardens and paused outside the door.

The monk turned as they entered. He wore his hood up and bowed at her presence. "Good eve, your majesty."

Vivienne stared at him, her brow arched. "A monk?" Her posture softened. "To what do I owe this visit."

Henry remained beside the door watching the interaction prepared to act should the need arise. His hand rested steadily on the hilt of his sword.

The monk reached up and lowered his hood. Even in the dim shadows of the garden, his deformities stood stark in contrast to the man he once was. It completely hid any defining features indicating by sight alone that this man was Francis.

To her credit, Vivienne contained her reaction to the mere flex of her hands against the folds of her skirt. Her expression remained demure and impassive.

"Do you not recognize me?" the scarred monk asked, his voice cracking with emotion. "Mother."

Vivienne stepped closer, searching his face. After a moment, she reached out a tentative hand and cupped his face. His eyes drifted closed at the touch. Silent tears slipped down her cheeks and her lip trembled as she caressed his cheek.

"Francis." She whispered his name softly as though he would vanish before her with a mere breath. "You are alive?"

He took her hand in his. "Aye."

"All this time, we believed you were dead. Stolen from us by the flames." She embraced him and the moment drew out in silence. When she finally stepped back, her joy radiated in her smile. "You must tell us everything."

Henry cleared his throat, and she spun around at the sound. "My lady, the king does not know of his return."

Her eyes widened with understanding. She pressed her lips into a thin line. "I see."

"Shall I summon him?" Henry nearly choked on the question knowing full well such a reunion would cause Crispin to lose restraint of his temper.

"Aye, but perhaps we should adjourn to somewhere more hospitable first?" Vivienne inhaled deeply. "My solar shall do nicely. Please meet us there directly."

"As you command, ma'am," Henry bowed allowing her to take Francis's arm and lead him from the garden.

Henry steeled himself for the inevitable battle looming on the horizon. There would be no way to hide this news from Crispin. All they could do was mitigate the damage it caused. He harbored no delusions concerning the upheaval such a revelation would create throughout the kingdom.

He wove through the corridors and down the staircase leading to the dining hall. Outside the hall, Henry paused at the sound of Crispin's voice. He braced his hand on the stone wall and took several fortifying breaths. Nothing could stop what was coming. Best to swing the blade now and suffer the consequences with honor.

Across the hall, he spotted a maid carrying a tray. Her chestnut hair peeked from under the cap she wore. Those mesmerizing green eyes locked on his from across the room. Her lips parted before forming a sweet smile. *Ivy.*

She ducked her head demurely and placed the tray on the head table.

Henry's attention shifted to Crispin and Ruby, who were engaged in conversation. When he returned his gaze to Ivy, she had already left the hall. Damn.

He would find Ivy later if he survived the awaiting skirmish.

Pushing away from the wall, Henry entered the room and strode directly to the table where Crispin sat.

"My liege." He bowed.

Crispin fixed him with a curious stare and laced his fingers with Ruby's. Her attention shifted between them. "I see you have returned. Have you news?" He kissed his wife's fingertips, making her blush.

Henry cleared his throat. "I beg your pardon, sire. But might we speak privately?"

"Nonsense. Whatever news you bring can be shared here." Crispin's lips curved in a lazy smile.

"The monk has returned with me." Henry straightened to his full height. "He wishes for an audience."

Ruby pulled her hand from Crispin's. "Deceiver," she hissed at Crispin. "I told you. The monk is no one."

Henry bit his tongue. "Sire, he awaits your presence in the solar."

Crispin rose to his feet and snatched Ruby's hand. "Let us not keep him waiting." Together they strode from the hall with Henry lagging behind.

Henry sent a silent prayer to heaven. If he survived this night, 'twould be a miracle.

Chapter Six

Fury and dread churned in the pit of Ruby's stomach. Crispin sent Henry to confront Brother James. He harbored no faith in her admission. Nay, in truth, she provided no falsehoods, no deception. She confessed without hesitation for she had nothing to hide.

Crispin's grip on her hand tightened. They marched down the corridors until they reached the solar where Vivienne spent much of her time. Why would they be meeting here instead of the king's presence chamber? She pushed the question aside and attempted to draw her hand from his when they reached the door to the solar. He held her firmly.

"Release me," she hissed through her teeth.

He turned, pinning her in place with the intensity of his stare and the set of his jaw. Ruby could not push against the stone of his resolve. She swallowed the bile biting the back of her throat and held his gaze afraid she may crumble beneath his scrutiny. He commanded her compliance without a single word. She wanted to fight against it, but if he ascertained the truth for himself by confirming her statement, then she would be justified. With a curt nod, she relented.

His attention shifted to Henry who stood silently behind them. Without a word, Crispin released her hand and opened the door, stepping aside and allowing her to enter first.

Brother James and Vivienne sat comfortably beside the fire chatting quietly. Ruby's presence brought the monk to his feet. He wore no hood, bearing his scars for the world to witness. A pang of guilt shot through her.

"Brother James, how good of you to grace us with your presence." She folded her hands in her lap to keep them from trembling.

"Ma'am." He bowed gracefully. Upon rising, his gaze shifted to the men behind her. "Your majesty." The monk bowed lower in supplication to her husband.

Crispin stepped forward, his blue eyes narrowed in calculation while skimming over the man before him. "My queen tells me of the vital work done by your monastery." He clasped his hands behind his back. "How noble."

"I am merely the Lord's humble servant." Brother James lifted his gaze to follow Crispin as he paced.

Ruby stood silent, her heart beating furiously in her breast. Henry remained beside her. His presence granted her some semblance of comfort, but still, she worried for the monk. Even Vivienne seemed hesitant to come between the two men as they took measure of each other.

"The Lord's servant?" Crispin scoffed. "Are you not also the king's loyal subject as well?"

Before the monk could respond, Vivienne interjected. "Enough with this petty display." She turned to Brother James. "Tell him."

"What is this, mother?" Crispin snapped, irritation giving a sharp edge to his tone.

"Do you not recognize him?" Vivienne's lips trembled. "Look closely."

"All I see is a scarred man of God." He curled his lip in a sneer.

Ruby longed to rage against his disrespectful remark. Henry's hand on her arm brought her to a halt. He gently shook his head. She refrained, instead focusing on the tension brewing in the room.

"Tell him," Vivienne prompted again, standing firm beside their guest.

"After all this time, you still have not learned the value of patience and respect. Have you, brother?" The monk's expression remained fixed, but his words sparked fury in Crispin who bared his teeth.

"Brother? You dare call me brother." He drew a blade from his hip and pressed it to the monk's throat. "My brother is dead.

You must think me a fool to think you are my blood."

"Crispin." Vivienne rested her hand on his arm. "Search your heart. 'Tis a miracle. Francis has returned."

Ruby swayed at the news and clutched at Henry's arm for support. She glanced at him for confirmation. The pale countenance and solid press of his lips together gave her little comfort but reaffirmed the claim. Could this monk truly be his long-lost brother? The rightful heir to the kingdom of Meradin.

He wrenched his arm from his mother's hold. "No." With determined steps, he pushed the monk until his back collided with the wall. "This man is not my brother. Francis is dead!" He spat the last words as though voicing them would make them manifest.

"Yes, the man you speak of is dead. I am no longer the brother you once knew." The monk spoke softly and with no fear for his own life. "He perished in the flames. Thanks to the monks in the monastery, I survived and was reborn from the ashes. My life is the Lord's, to serve him in all things."

Ruby clutched at her throat. The man did not even attempt to plead for his own life. How could Crispin not show mercy to his brother? She knew of their complicated history, but such a revelation should bring joy unless it shattered the stability of the kingdom. Her heart broke at the sight of her husband in fury and torment, knowing the battle waging inside his soul.

Crispin dug the blade into the scarred flesh, his hand clenched in the dark robes pinning the man to the wall. "Why have you returned?" He shook the monk. "Have you come to claim your title?"

Francis slowly raised his hands in supplication. "I have no quarrel with you, brother. I come bearing only goodwill and peace."

Crispin hissed and ground his teeth. With a pained shout, he released Francis and stepped back. The blade remained firmly planted in his fist, ready to strike should the need arise.

The monk slumped against the wall, sliding his hand against his throat where the blade nicked his flesh. "I beg your forgiveness, 'twas not my intention to cause you concern or create upheaval."

"Why have you come then?" Crispin's question cut to the heart of the beast.

"Henry discovered the truth and requested I no longer hide it. I bore a responsibility to reveal myself to both you and our mother." His gaze held Ruby's for a moment before he turned to Vivienne. "I longed to tell you, but in revealing my existence, I have unleashed chaos."

Ruby's heart ached at his words. He wished to live out his days in obscurity and peace, but this revelation would shake the kingdom, threatening the foundation of all they knew.

A shadow crossed Crispin's face. "Aye. And now I must find a way to contain it." With a growl, he spun around to face Henry. "Find a suitable room and lock him in it."

Henry's jaw flexed, but he inclined his head in acknowledgment. "As you command, sire."

"You cannot imprison him!" Ruby held her tongue long enough. Such a response proved unwarranted. She grabbed Crispin's arm, forcing him to face her. "He is your brother!"

His crystalline blue eyes pierced her soul. "Precisely the reason he must remain here, out of sight."

Ruby recoiled as though he struck her. "You would imprison a man simply for telling the truth?"

"I will do what is necessary to keep the kingdom of Meradin from descending into chaos." He sheathed his blade and snatched Francis by the arm. "Come, allow me to escort you personally."

Tears pricked her eyes. She turned her gaze to Francis. "Please forgive me."

"There is nothing to forgive, my queen." He cast a forlorn glance at Vivienne. "All will be well, mother."

Vivienne took Ruby's hand and drew her into her embrace as Henry and Crispin led Francis from the solar. Her hold tightened around Ruby as their footsteps faded down the hall.

Ruby wanted to charge after them, throw herself on his mercy to beg for the monk's release, but Crispin made his position quite clear. She could not present an argument without investigation. Oh, what folly.

"Breathe, my dear. Breathe." Vivienne's touch soothed her even as the rage simmered like molten steel beneath her flesh.

"How could he imprison his own brother?" Ruby demanded. She fisted her hands in the soft fabric of Vivienne's gown. "Heartless bastard!"

Violence poured through her. The need to purge it made her physically ill. Ruby pulled free of Vivienne's embrace and spilled the contents of her stomach on the floor. Her body trembled with every heave. She wiped her hand across her mouth and steadied herself against the wall.

"My child." Vivienne's warm touch against her back gave her little comfort. "Come, you should sit." She led her to a chair beside the fire. "Remain here. I shall return in a moment."

Ruby rested her head in her hands and closed her eyes. The wave of sickness abated slowly. She focused on the sound of the wood cracking in the fire and slowing the rapid thundering of her heart against her ribs.

Brother James was Francis. This revelation could certainly cast the country into turmoil should it come to light. But Francis assured Crispin he had no designs on the crown. Even so, it changed nothing. He would need to officially abdicate the throne to silence any dissent against Crispin's rightful claim. She groaned at the thought of what might transpire should it not find an adequate resolution.

What of her? What of the child she carried? Her heart plunged into the icy depths of uncertainty. Ruby shivered at the possible consequences of such a struggle.

Vivienne returned with several servants, one of whom carried a steaming mug.

Ruby accepted it without question while the other servants cleaned the mess she made. Her face heated in shame. She could clean it herself, but Vivienne would never allow it. Instead, she sipped the contents of the earthen mug in her hands.

A gentle herbal tea. It settled her stomach and warmed her body.

Vivienne sat beside her. They remained silent until the

servants finished and left them alone.

"Do not fret, my dear." Vivienne's attention shifted from the fire to Ruby. "This is Crispin's way. He will come to his senses."

"How can you be certain?" Ruby clutched the mug tighter in her hands.

She lifted her shoulder in an airy shrug. "He is my son. They both are. They have always been at odds with one another."

"Are you not concerned for Francis's welfare?" Ruby stared at her in confusion.

"Crispin may be impulsive, but he knows I will not tolerate cruelty." Vivienne straightened and their gazes locked. "His fears are founded."

Ruby hung her head. "But to treat his brother with such unveiled animosity is in itself a vicious punishment."

Vivienne sighed. "As overjoyed as I am at the news of my firstborn's survival, this news brings with it a complex web of uncertainties. It certainly overshadows any other joyful revelations." Her pointed look made Ruby flinch.

"Aye." Ruby sipped her tea, purposefully avoiding her gaze.

"You have not told him of your condition." Vivienne's words held no censure, but she felt the sting of it nonetheless.

"I intended to tell him this night." Ruby shifted in the chair.

"Perhaps it would be prudent to wait a few days." Her words gave voice to Ruby's thoughts.

"It would be wise indeed." Ruby agreed.

The heavy burden of keeping the secret longer pulled tight around her, smothering and suffocating with its weight. While she did not relish the thought of telling him she carried his child, it seemed the implications of her revelation would only complicate matters. She had no way of knowing if he would be pleased or angered by her state.

"Finish your tea, my dear." Vivienne rested her hand on Ruby's. "For this eve, all you can do is rest. There will be time to worry on the morrow."

"What of Crispin?" Ruby asked, longing for some resolution, some peace of mind.

"He is as strong as he is stubborn." Vivienne offered a comforting smile. "Give him wide berth this eve. If he seeks you out, be patient. Remember, you were originally betrothed to Francis. If he loses the throne, he loses you. The battle waging inside him must be brutal and unrelenting."

Unable to form a response, Ruby finished her tea. The words repeated over and over in her mind. *If he loses the throne, he loses you.*

Even though she was furious with Crispin, she still loved him. Regardless of his behavior, he was her husband and her king. Loyalty formed a strong bond, one she was unwilling to break. There must be a solution suitable to all parties involved which did not involve bloodshed.

Vivienne accompanied her to her chamber and bid her good night.

As she lay in the dark, she whispered a prayer for Crispin's soul, hoping it was not too late to salvage what remained.

Chapter Seven

The fire crackled in the hearth, and a log split, spitting sparks and hissing. Crispin surrendered himself to the flames. A goblet dangled from his fingertips. He glanced at the tankard of wine sitting on the table beside him. There was not enough wine in the kingdom to drown the thoughts buffeting his mind like a battering ram. Slouched in the oversized chair, he downed the remaining wine in his cup.

After leaving their unexpected guest in Henry's capable hands, Crispin retreated to his chamber, demanding wine and solitude.

God's blood, teeth, and bones. His brother was alive. Scarred almost beyond recognition, and yet he glimpsed a shadow of his brother beneath the tight, mangled flesh. Francis had been handsome, more so than Crispin to some. He mirrored their father's fair looks and classical profile while Crispin favored his mother's family with their dark hair and sleek, hawkish features. It seemed the fire he once assumed stole his brother's life only stole his appearance.

The thought enraged him. Not because he wished his brother ill, but because his return heralded a new threat. A viable challenge to Crispin's place as King of Meradin.

Surprise and fury raged through him. He contained himself quite admirably upon receiving the news. It took a lion's share of restraint not to unleash his wrath upon Francis. Embracing the darkness would have been a simple task. But one glance at his queen gave him pause.

Her lovely face bore not only the evidence of her shock at the revelation, it pleaded for mercy. No matter what bloodlust thundered through him, he could not tarnish what tenuous threads remained in their fragile reunion.

He raked his hand over his face and slammed the goblet down on the table nearly upsetting the tankard. What recourse remained?

Killing the monk, his brother, crossed his mind, but he shoved the thought aside. Revulsion stung his conscience at the thought. Ruby, Henry, and especially his mother, would revile him for such a wicked act.

His stomach twisted at the thought of bringing Francis before the Privy Council. While it would be the most diplomatic and regal decision, Crispin detested the thought of his fate resting in their greedy hands. Nay, he must consider his next move carefully before action. He needed to speak to Francis alone before making a decision on which path to take.

But such a delicate conversation would have to wait until the morrow. Crispin was in no state to discuss anything of such importance while his blood ran hot. He scowled into the fire watching the flames lick the stone, scorching it with black lashes of soot and ash.

Transported to another time, Crispin wallowed in the memory. He stood helpless watching the flames rise high into the night sky. The building consumed by the inferno slowly crumbled, revealing the skeleton of smoldering beams. Henry beside him, pacing and shouting for the villagers to escape to a safe distance.

Crispin absorbed the heat as it pulsed from the inn. Just moments before he watched his brother dash into the building when someone told him there were others trapped inside. Francis never hesitated. He disappeared into the flames. Crispin held his breath, rooted to the spot, whether from cowardice or self-preservation, it mattered not.

When the building collapsed, Crispin's shout was engulfed by the thunder of the crunching timbers and hiss of the flames. Francis was gone. Or so he believed.

How had he survived? Nothing survived that inferno. Nothing.

It was not until later they discovered several knights, Simon, Timothy, and Jacob, had been trapped in the inn as well as a family with three young children. Every soul perished. All but one, it seemed.

A miracle. A blessing. Crispin's mood darkened. "A curse," he muttered beneath his breath.

The fire cracked in response.

A knock at the door disentangled him from his haunted memories.

"Go away!"

"Sire." Henry's voice came muffled through the wood.

"Leave me," Crispin growled, wishing for nothing but solitude.

The door hinges creaked. "Sire." Henry entered his chamber.

Crispin tightened his grip on the goblet. "Have you no care for your life? I said I do not wish to be disturbed."

"I cannot abandon you in such a state." Henry approached like a faithful but wary hound.

"Can you not follow instructions?" He tilted his head to meet his loyal companion's gaze.

"I beg your pardon?" Concern creased Henry's brow.

"I send you on a simple errand, and you return with ruin in your wake." Crispin slowly rose to his feet.

Henry stepped back. "I did only as you commanded."

"My command was to uncover the connection between my queen and this mysterious monk." He clenched his teeth. "Instead, you return my sainted brother brought back from the dead."

"Would you rather I hide this knowledge from you? From your mother?" Henry stood his ground, his eyes ablaze and jaw firmly set.

"I would rather have left the past buried." Crispin jabbed a finger in Henry's chest.

Henry rounded on him, forcing him back several paces. "I will not play conspirator to hide the truth. If you do not wish to embrace your brother's return, so be it. But I will not allow you to thrust the kingdom into discord because it displeases you to have your brother return."

"I am your king." Crispin grabbed a fistful of Henry's tunic. "You will do as I command or suffer the penalty of treason."

Wrenching himself from Crispin's grasp, Henry rested his hand on the pommel of his sword.

A throaty chuckle burst from Crispin's chest. "Aye. Draw your sword." He withdrew his own and held it between them. "Do it."

Unable to back down, Henry drew his blade. Crispin swung, bringing his crashing against Henry's in a ringing bite of steel against steel. They slid together until the hilts collided, drawing the men closer.

Determination marred Henry's brow. His eyes flashed with panic and fury. "I do not wish to fight you."

"Coward." Crispin shifted his weight and knocked the sword from Henry's hand. It clattered to the floor.

When Henry lunged for it, Crispin kicked it away. He placed himself firmly between the two. "Will you not even defend yourself?"

Without hesitation, he brought the blade down, nearly striking Henry's shoulder. But his companion moved swiftly, ducking out of his reach and spinning around.

"Fight me!" Blood pounded through Crispin, driving him with the need to break something. Anything.

Henry barreled forward with a shout, driving his body into Crispin's and knocking him back into the wall. The sword flew from his hand and skidded across the floor.

His eyes ablaze, Henry drove his fist into Crispin's side. He retaliated, wresting his arms free and shoving his opponent away. Henry swung his fist.

Crispin tried to avoid the blow, but it caught him on the side of the face. His head spun. He drew back and landed two blows to Henry's face causing blood to spurt from his nose.

"Fuck." Henry spat on the floor and charged forward, knocking the wind from Crispin as they tumbled to the ground.

In a flurry of wailing fists and ribald curses, Henry pinned Crispin to the ground with his arm to his throat. Blood smeared across his face, running over his jaw and dripping onto Crispin's tunic.

Crispin's heart pounded. The metallic taste of blood filled his mouth. Rage pulsed through his veins with every labored breath. Henry's weight doubled the effort it took to breathe and silenced his ability to speak.

"Enough," Henry spat. "Enough." He withdrew and staggered as he stood.

Crispin gasped for air. The release of pressure brought stars to his vision. He lay a moment, staring at the wooden beams on the ceiling, his thoughts scattered. Finally, he pushed himself to his feet and stumbled to the table where his goblet sat. He poured some wine and offered it to Henry.

With a wary glance, he accepted it and drank deeply before shoving the goblet back at Crispin.

"Sit." Crispin poured himself a drink and collapsed in his chair.

Henry sat across from him. He pulled his tunic free and dabbed his nose with his sleeve to staunch the blood. They sat in silence for a few moments as the heat of their fight dissipated.

"I have many questions." Crispin gazed into the fire once more, willing his racing heart to slow. "But I fear the answers will bring me no comfort."

"Perhaps it would be wise to bring Francis before the council. He can explain the circumstances surrounding his absence." Henry's words were muffled beneath the bloody tunic, but they rang clearly enough to comprehend.

"And what shall I do when the council deems him to be the rightful King of Meradin?" Crispin allowed the darkness to consume him once more. "Shall I forfeit the crown and return to being the wastrel prince?"

"He does not want the crown. Or have you been too stubborn to comprehend the subtleties in his words?" Henry slouched and tipped his head back to rest it against the chair. "He returned in an effort to maintain peace should his existence be discovered."

The mere thought of Francis taking the crown ignited a simmering hatred in his gut. But it stoked into a hellish inferno at the possibility of him taking possession of Ruby. He snorted in disgust.

"You believe him to still be the sainted man you once knew. Beneath the piety and righteous cloak of Godly service, he is still a man. One with desires."

"God's teeth," Henry swore and leaned forward dropping the cloth from his face. The blood smeared across the lower half of his face and down his neck. "Do you think he would throw himself upon your mercy now only to demand the crown and cast you into the pit?"

"He. Is. A. Man." Crispin enunciated each word clearly, holding Henry's gaze steadily. "A man of flesh and blood. And I will not relinquish what is mine."

Henry studied his face for a few long moments. "This is not about the crown."

Crispin tossed back the wine, letting it burn to the pit of his stomach, and poured another.

"Ruby." Her name on his lips made every hair on Crispin's neck rise with a prickling awareness. He turned to stare into the flames unable to bear the scrutiny. Try as he might, he could not hide his visceral reaction to her. Ruby belonged to him. No one, save the Almighty himself, would steal her away from him.

A soft chuckle brought Crispin's attention back to his companion. He scowled. Was his weakness so evident? If it were so clear to Henry, then the entire kingdom would know how much he valued this one woman.

"Would you give up the crown to save Ruby?" Henry's question broke through the haze of his twisted thoughts. "If given the choice between keeping the throne and keeping your love, which would you sacrifice?"

Crispin shot to his feet and tossed the goblet across the room. He raked his hand through his hair and gripped the stone mantel over the hearth. Such a question should not throw him into torment. The throne was his. It had always been his dream, his destiny. But that was before he found Ruby, before he discovered the light she brought to his darkness. Her passion and bravery unveiled a brilliance unsurpassed by any treasure in all the world. The thought of losing such an exquisite gem, a part of his very soul, tortured him.

"You cannot ask this of me." Crispin's response echoed in the chamber. He turned to face the only man he trusted with his life, his brother not by blood, but by shared sacrifice and sacred vow. "I will never relinquish my throne nor my queen."

Henry's heavy sigh sank into his bones. He could not expect his longstanding friend to understand the severity of the situation nor the consequences of revealing a scrap of weakness. This was his burden to bear alone, and he would fight to keep the kingdom and Ruby within his grasp.

"What would you have me do, sire?" Henry rose and crossed to where Crispin stood. He clapped his hand on Crispin's shoulder.

"I shall decide on the morrow." Crispin mimicked the action making Henry wince. "Go take your pleasure. Rest. But think no more on it this night."

"I am your servant, sire." Henry bowed and took up his sword laying along the far wall. Without a word, he nodded and left the room.

Alone once more, Crispin turned back to the fire and lost himself in thought. What would the morning bring? He closed his eyes. The ache in his heart and his loins begged him to seek comfort. *Ruby*. His cock hardened at the thought of her. As much as he wanted to bury himself in her warmth and seek refuge, he knew she would refuse him.

After the confrontation with Francis, Ruby would hold him at bay. Mercy would be construed as weakness. Little did she know, his actions toward his brother were merciful. Her presence prodded his restraint. If he had his way, his brother would be packed out on the next ship to the furthest destination he could find. If he truly wished to live in service to God, it would not matter where he served.

But his conscience could not bear the weight of his mother and Ruby's censure toward his reckless actions. He loved them both and would not suffer such silent torment.

There would be no peace until he found a suitable

compromise. But how could he possibly compete with his brother, the saint and servant of God? He pinched the bridge of his nose. *God's blood, teeth, and bones.*

The council would revel in Francis's return and cast Crispin aside, unless he could convince Francis to abdicate his claim to the throne officially before the privy council, in the sight of everyone and before God. Only then would Crispin secure his kingdom and the woman he loved.

Chapter Eight

Between the exhaustion caused by the events of the day and the throbbing pain in his head, Henry desired nothing but sleep. He knew better than to confront Crispin in such a state. But part of his responsibility, as both friend and the right hand of the king, was to mitigate any possible conflicts.

Francis's miraculous return certainly provided cause for celebration, but it also provided its own share of conflicts. Crispin took the news better than he could have hoped. He dabbed his hand against his nose and flinched as the pain shot through him. Truth be told, he expected bloodshed or at the very least, banishment. He would suffer a broken nose and shattered pride if it saved the kingdom a strap of conflict. The people deserved better.

As he walked the silent corridors, his mind churned with possibilities. What would the council say? What would Crispin do? As of this moment, there was not much he could influence. Fate must run its course.

He rounded the corner and spied a figure emerging from the king's presence chamber. The figure stepped into the torchlight, illuminating chestnut curls tucked beneath a maid's cap and a sinful figure clothed in a simple woolen gown.

"Ivy." All thoughts fled his mind.

She spun at the sound of her name, pressing her back against the wall. "Your grace." She dipped into a curtsey.

Henry rushed forward but paused at Ivy's gasp.

"Your face." Her gentle touch against his cheek set his heart alight. "What happened?"

"Oh, training," he lied, pulling her into his arms. He ached for her since that night. The tenderness in her voice nearly brought him to his knees. "My sweet girl. Where have you been hiding?" He pressed a kiss to her palm.

Rose pink blossomed across her cheeks. "I visited my family. Mother was ill."

"I searched the castle for days." He trailed kisses along the inside of her wrist. "When I left with the king, I feared I would never see your beautiful face again."

She swayed into his touch. "I should have told you."

"Come with me." He laced their fingers together and pulled her along the corridors. She followed willingly, her grip tight in his.

When they reached his chamber, he locked the door behind them. She slid her arms around his waist and pressed her lips to his.

The force of his kiss drew a whimper from deep within her. She clung to him, as desperate for his touch as he was for hers. When he drew back, he cringed at the sight of his blood smeared across her face.

"Damn." He snatched a clean cloth from the washbasin filled with fresh water and wiped the blood from her face.

She took the cloth from his hand and pointed to the bed. "Sit."

Henry followed her instructions. She tipped his chin up and gently cleaned his face. Her bright eyes intent with focus as she worked. The soft brush of her fingertips against his skin drove his concerns into the forgotten recesses of his mind. In this moment, there was only Ivy.

He rested his hands on the backs of her thighs, drawing her closer. She rinsed the cloth and cleaned his cheeks down onto his neck.

"Remove your doublet and tunic." Her words rang with authority.

Henry's cock sprang to attention. He obeyed without question, slowly drawing the items from his body and dropping them onto the floor.

A smile tugged at Ivy's lips as she rinsed the rag and ran the damp cloth over his torso.

"And the rest." Her gaze dropped to his lower half.

Without breaking her gaze, he rose enough to push his hose

down and dispensed with whatever clothing remained.

Ivy licked her lips at the sight of him. His cock grew at her appreciative perusal.

He grasped her thighs and gathered the fabric of her skirts in his fists. The rag slipped from her hands and her breaths quickened as he drew the skirt up to her waist. When he tugged her down so she straddled his thighs, her sweet cunt nestled perfectly against his aching cock. He basked in the slide of her wet heat against him.

"Henry." She took his face between her palms and kissed him. Her body rocked against his.

He fit himself to her and drove inside her welcoming body. Ivy's nails dug into his shoulders as he thrust deep. Her warmth surrounded him, her cunt gripping him tight.

Lost in the blissful heat, Henry gripped her by the waist. "I have missed you, Ivy."

She bucked her hips against him, finding a movement that brought their bodies together in delightful friction. He held her tight as she rode him, and he met her rhythm with his thrusts.

Her cap fell from her head, and her curls tumbled free. Henry admired the gentle curve of her throat, her soft parted lips. Their mingled moans echoed off his chamber walls.

Together they lost themselves in the heat and their own animalistic need. Henry felt her body tighten against him as her climax drew closer. He drove harder and faster until she cried out and her cunt pulsed around his cock. His release barreled toward him at a full gallop. He threw his head back and cursed as he came.

Ivy rested her head against his shoulder and purred in contentment. After a few moments, she slowly stood.

"Stay." Henry took her hand. "Please."

Hesitation flickered in her green eyes. "If that is what you wish."

"Of course." He stood, turning her, and slowly unlaced her gown, kissing her skin as he revealed it. "Is there someone else waiting for you?"

"N-no." She whimpered. Her garments fell, encircling her

feet.

Henry snaked his arm around her waist and pulled her flush against him. His cock nestled against the cleft of her backside. With every sweet kiss he planted along her shoulder, his fingertips journeyed across her bare stomach.

"Then tell me, sweet girl. Why are you so eager to flee my presence?" He nipped her ear lobe, tugging it between his teeth.

"I—" Her voice drifted into a moan as his fingers slid between her folds. Her hips arched against his touch.

"Are you not satisfied?" He languidly stroked her, drawing their pleasure back to the surface as well as the truth.

"Aye." She gasped and writhed in his embrace as he quickened his pace.

"Why were you in the king's presence chamber?" His touch never wavered, but Ivy stilled at his question. He held her steady in case she attempted to pull from his embrace. "Do not lie to me, my sweet. You are at my mercy."

Her breaths came quicker. His fingertips made languid circles around her swollen nub. The silence stretched tight, but Henry stood firm. He would have her secrets. Every. Last. One.

"I was searching for you." Her quivering voice echoed in the small room. "Please." She squirmed her hips, seeking release.

Henry pondered her reply while drawing out her torment. "Why did you not come to me sooner?"

"I dare not risk the king's displeasure." Ivy rested her hands on his bare hips, digging her nails into his flesh drawing him closer, grinding her backside against him. "I needed to complete my evening tasks before…" The words disappeared on a panting moan.

Henry spun her in his arms and stared deep into her bewitching eyes. "Before what?"

Her dazed smile drew his attention to her mouth. Passion painted her skin a lovely shade of pink. She licked her lips and touched his jaw with reverence. "Before I sought my pleasure."

Having her in his arms and his bed fulfilled his deepest desires. Every night, he dreamed of her, woke hard for the want of her. Women threw themselves upon him during his travels, but he shunned them for they never compared to the beauty who ensnared his heart.

Even so, he proceeded with hesitation. Ivy, as enticing as she was, could prove to be a distraction to his duties. He knew nothing of her past or her family. A pretty enticement to keep him from his king and his vow to the service of the crown. He pushed aside the insistent demands of his cock and instead focused on the woman before him with single-minded determination.

Her brow furrowed. "Have I offended you, your grace?"

"How long have you been a servant in the castle?" The question burst from him without thought.

"Three summers." She maintained her poise while gently caressing his jaw.

This meant little to him since he spent much of that time traveling at the command of the late king. He had no means to verify her claim.

"What is your position here?" He held her gaze, searching for any sign of deceit.

"I serve as the queen's personal maid." She frowned. "Why do you look at me so?"

He smoothed his hands over the small of her back, keeping her close. "I find myself quite uncertain when it comes to you." He inhaled deeply, savoring the scent of her. "You drive me to madness, and I cannot purge you from my mind."

"I find myself in the same position," Ivy confessed. She cupped the back of his head and drew him closer rising to capture his lips in a heady kiss. "'Tis my duty to care for the queen. Even more so now that she is with child."

Henry froze. The words seeped through the fog of desire and doused him with cold water. He pulled back, holding Ivy at a distance so he could think clearly. "The queen is with child?"

The passion fled Ivy's face, leaving it pale. She clapped her hand over her mouth. "Forgive me. I vowed I would not reveal it." Ivy buried her face in her hands. "The queen will cast me out. I have failed." A sob wracked her.

"Do not fret." Henry drew her into his embrace. Her tears

fell hot against his skin. "I shall not reveal your secret." Even as he comforted Ivy, the revelation circled in his mind. This changed everything.

Should Crispin discover this, he would do all in his power to secure his claim to the throne. What would that mean for Francis? Dread settled in the pit of his stomach. How could he possibly conceal such a secret from his friend? From his king? God's blood, if Crispin discovered he withheld this knowledge, he would face more than a mere bruised face. He would face the tip of the king's sword.

Ivy clung to him, her sobs slowly fading. She drew back, and he met her tearful gaze with an ache in his breast. He brushed his thumb across the streaks marring her lovely face.

He kissed her swollen lips and drew her into his bed. There he made love to her, whispering sweet words in her ear, promises of protection and passion. When they were both sated, he drew her against him in his narrow bed.

Her soft slumbering breaths brought him comfort. For too long he spent his time alone. Having this companionship with Ivy brought him joy, no matter how fleeting it may be.

He burrowed closer to her warmth, entwining their legs together. When he closed his eyes to sleep, he pondered the truth of Ivy's revelation.

Ruby carried Crispin's child. This should be cause for celebration. Why has Ruby not told Crispin the wonderful news?

Broken memories flashed through his mind. Ruby. Bound and blindfolded. At their mercy. His mouth and hands on her skin. He inhaled sharply. While most of that night lay shrouded in alcohol-induced darkness, he remembered Crispin's words vividly. He used him to satisfy his sexual desires.

Could it be possible the child was not Crispin's, but Henry's? The thought alone left Henry in a cold sweat. He clung tighter to Ivy, who slumbered on oblivious to the chaos surrounding the kingdom of Meradin threatening to tear it apart.

Chapter Nine

After a sleepless night spent alone, Ruby came to the realization the only way she would get any answers would be to ask them directly, even if it meant defying the king's command.

Ruby approached the two guards standing outside a room in the western wing of the castle. They straightened at her presence.

"Your majesty." They bowed and spoke in unison.

"I have come to speak with the monk." Ruby attempted to portray confidence in her statement but feared they would see through her.

The guards shifted their stance to block the door. "We cannot allow that, your majesty."

"Under whose authority?" She pinned them with her most regal stare.

"The king." The shorter guard acknowledged.

"Is this man a prisoner?" She folded her hands and held her ground.

The guards glanced at each other but did not answer.

"Then he is a guest." She gestured toward the room behind them. "And as the queen, I have every right to speak with him."

"But, your majesty…" The taller guard hesitated even as the shorter one stepped aside.

"Has the king given explicit instructions to keep me from speaking with our guest?" She held his gaze even though her stomach fluttered.

Relenting, the guard stepped aside. "Would you like us to accompany you, your majesty?"

"That will not be necessary. He is a man of God, not a criminal." She pushed open the door and entered the small chamber, ensuring it closed firmly behind her.

Francis knelt beside the bed, his head bowed in prayer. In all their years of acquaintance, she had no reason to believe him to be anything but a loyal servant of God. But when he revealed his past, it transformed his entire life. Just as her past had come to light and altered her destiny.

"You humble me with your presence, my queen." The man before her crossed himself and slowly rose to his feet. His scarred visage no longer startled her. He wore his hood down, unashamed of his appearance.

"I have come to apologize." Ruby gestured to the chair. "May I sit?"

He nodded and sat on the bed across from her. "You do not need to ask for my permission or apologize. You are the queen." His friendly smile soothed her.

"After the way Crispin treated you last eve, I must apologize." She interlaced her fingers and dropped her gaze. "I should have defended you."

"You defended me valiantly, my queen. I cannot hold my brother's sins against his lovely bride." Francis's words made her face heat.

"Why did you not tell me the truth of your identity?" Her curiosity defeated her courtesy. "Had you no faith in me?"

"It has nothing to do with my faith in you." He waved his hand. "Until Henry arrived at the monastery, I told no one of my past or my true identity. After I survived the fire, I took it as a sign from God to dedicate my life to my true purpose."

"I cannot help but think my actions have led you to this point." Ruby warred with her guilt in an attempt to offer consolation and support. "If it were not for me, they would never have discovered the truth and left you in peace."

"The truth would have come to light in due course," Francis assured her, but it did little to ease her conscience. "Your visits brought hope to the monastery and those who rely on our work. Do not harbor regret. 'Tis all part of God's great plan."

His humility struck her. "Allow me to petition on your behalf. I am sure we can find an arrangement for you to return to the monastery and be allowed to continue your mission."

Francis shook his head. "I have decided to remain here and heal the broken bond between myself and my brother. I owe him that much."

The thoughtful consideration for Crispin, even though his actions were abhorrent, left Ruby speechless. Francis bore no ill will toward his brother and sincerely wished for healing. How vastly different were these brothers' temperaments. It held her in awe as they conversed.

"Do you think such a break can be mended?" she asked. "Crispin has a tendency to be quite stubborn."

His warm laughter filled the room. "It has always been one of Crispin's more prominent traits. But I believe the Lord can make use of even our most egregious faults."

"Becoming king has not corrected these faults, I fear." Ruby sighed.

"A man cannot change who he is unless he embraces his faults and seeks to improve himself." Francis folded his hands together, tucking them inside the sleeves of his robes. "'For all have sinned and fallen short of the glory of God.'"

"Amen." Ruby bowed her head in reverence. When she lifted her gaze, Francis studied her, his blue gaze intense. "Is something amiss?"

"He has found a bountiful treasure in you, Ruby." His words touched her soul. "Any man would be blessed beyond measure to have you by his side."

She shifted in her seat, unsure how to respond to his compliment.

He cocked his head. "You seem conflicted."

His astute observation left her stunned. "I…am." Ruby inhaled deep allowing her thoughts to settle before responding. "As the queen, 'tis my responsibility to ensure the people of Meradin are protected and prosperous."

"And yet you doubt your abilities to provide this security." He countered. "Why?"

Silence filled the room as she searched for an answer. None came. Doubt rose unbidden from the dark reaches of her mind.

"Crispin." His name fell from her lips. "I find myself torn

between my love for him and my duty to my people."

Francis's smile disappeared with a nod. "I see. Do you feel choosing one is a betrayal to the other?"

"In a strange way, that seems the most plausible explanation." Ruby studied his features. Even beneath the scars, she saw the strong line of his jaw. A shadow of the handsome prince hidden beneath the scarred surface.

He would have been king, if not for the fire. If not for Crispin. The realization made her pause. Had her caravan not been attacked and Francis not been caught in the flames, they would have been wed. That had been the original betrothal agreement. Francis, the firstborn son of King Edgar and Queen Vivienne of Meradin, and Eleanor, daughter of King Henry V and Queen Katherine of England.

But fate intervened offering her a different path, even though the destination remained the same. On the throne of Meradin. Heat flooded her at Francis's curious gaze. She lost herself in thought and completely forgot herself.

"My apologies. I have intruded on your time long enough." She rose to her feet.

Francis also rose. "'Twas not an intrusion. I welcome our conversations." He bowed.

"I shall send some food and wine. You are our guest, not a prisoner." She opened the door.

Both guards stood before her, swords drawn, contradicting her words.

"God grant you mercy, my queen." Francis offered her a parting blessing.

The tall guard closed the door and stood sentry once more. Ruby shot him a parting glare and strode down the hallway. She rounded the corner and ran into a warm, but solid wall.

"Did you enjoy your visit with our guest?" Crispin hissed the last word between his teeth and grasped her wrist.

Before she could reply, he turned and strode down the hall, dragging her behind him. She sputtered and struggled to keep up with his pace, tripping over the hem of her skirts.

"Release me," she growled under her breath.

He ignored her demand and refused to stop until they reached her chamber. Crispin threw open the door and pulled her inside, slamming the door behind them.

She caught the bedpost and spun to glare at him. "How dare you treat me in such a manner?"

Crispin crossed the room and pinned her between his body and the bedpost. The heat of him and the blue fire blazing in his eyes struck her dumb as effectively as if he had slapped her.

"Did you sate your curiosity?" The control in his voice spoke louder than any punishment. Crispin was furious.

"He is not a prisoner. He is our guest." She tilted her chin up and met his gaze squarely. "And your brother."

"Oh yes," Crispin murmured, his hand coming to rest on her throat. The touch delicate, but imposing. "My brother. Sainted Francis. The golden prince."

Even though Ruby trembled beneath his touch, her body wept for him. *Jealousy.* The word formed on her tongue unbidden. She saw the truth of it in his eyes down into the very depths of his soul.

"You are jealous of Francis."

His jaw twitched. "I am not jealous of a scarred monk."

"Not the man you see now, the man as you remember him." She touched his cheek.

Crispin's hand dropped from her throat. He stepped back out of her reach. "You are forbidden to be alone with him. Is that understood?"

Rage burst inside her. "You have no right—"

"I have every right! I am your king! I am your husband! You will obey me in all things." Crispin's outburst shook the room. He flexed his hands at his sides, his eyes wide, hair wild.

Ruby stumbled away from him, wishing she had worn her dagger. She knew he would never hurt her, but this passion inside him rose from a darkness that left her trembling.

"Get out." She struggled to keep her voice steady.

"Ruby." Crispin raked his hand through his hair in frustration. He reached for her, but she withdrew, blocking his progress with a chair.

"Leave." Her lip trembled and tears pricked her eyes, but she refused to show weakness. Her heart ached to hold him, to soothe his wounded soul, but her pride refused to allow him the pleasure of her company after his incomprehensible actions.

Crispin's sky-blue gaze darkened like a summer tempest over the ocean. "As you wish." He bowed and wrenched open the door.

When it slammed behind him, Ruby collapsed to the floor burying her face in her hands. Sobs came in wave after wave, drawing on whatever remaining strength she possessed. She lay on the floor until it slowly subsided.

How could she have been so foolish? Crispin would never change. Not for her, not for the kingdom. His actions bore the same marks as the headstrong, self-indulgent bastard she saved that summer night outside the brothel. If anything, her conversation with Francis only solidified her fears.

She rested her hand on her stomach. How could she even bring a child into this world with such turmoil and uncertainty? Any resolution she hoped to find turned to ash. Crispin served himself, neither her nor their child would alter the path he set himself upon.

Ruby rose to her feet and leaned against the window, staring out beyond the bailey at the forest beyond the castle walls. Dark storm clouds clustered on the horizon. Helplessness filled her, and for the first time in years, Ruby prayed for guidance knowing God would never listen to a sinner's plea for absolution and mercy.

Chapter Ten

Henry woke to a warm, soft body curled around his. Even in his narrow bed, he relished the delightful surprise of finding Ivy still tucked against him. Her thigh draped across his, her head nestled against his chest. Her breath caressed his bare skin.

Ivy. A treasure among the thorns. She wove her way into his heart with her sweet smile and adventurous lovemaking. His heart ached at the thought of abandoning their small oasis. Since he found her, he had little intention of releasing her. He tightened his grip on the blanket binding them together.

Light filtered in through the narrow window. Morning had come against his wishes. He longed to linger with her, but if he knew anything, Crispin would send for him, demanding his presence immediately. Between the upcoming festival and Francis's unexpected arrival, there was much to be done.

He kissed the top of her head, inhaling deeply and committing her intoxicating scent to memory. She shifted, burrowing beneath the blanket as he slowly rose from the bed. Her soft moan made his cock stiffen. God's teeth, he wanted her again.

Quietly, he donned his garments and retrieved hers, draping them over the foot of the bed. Henry's gaze lingered on Ivy's sleeping form before he placed her bodice atop her skirt. His fingers brushed the seams. He frowned and glanced at the fabric. Was that parchment?

He inspected it, sliding his fingers along the stitching. The folds parted revealing a small pocket. Tucked inside lay a piece of faded parchment.

Curiosity consumed him. He unfolded it. Familiar writing painted the parchment followed by a royal seal. Confusion gave way to disbelief. Why would Ivy have this hidden in her possession?

"Henry." Ivy's sultry voice pulled him from his thoughts.

"What is the meaning of this?" Fury boiled in Henry's blood. He shoved the parchment forward. Her wide eyes narrowed on it.

"What is it?" Ivy rose from the bed, unashamed of her unclothed state. "I often find discarded items in the course of my duties and tuck them inside my bodice for safekeeping."

"This is no scrap. It bears the king's royal seal." He forced himself not to let his gaze wander down the length of her tempting curves. "Did you take this from the king's presence chamber?"

Ivy tilted her chin up, facing him directly without simpering or begging. She denied nothing, nor did she confess. They stood a breath apart, unmoving. "I do not remember where I found it."

Henry grabbed her arms. "Do not lie to me. I saw you leave the king's presence chamber last eve."

Her green eyes flashed with fire before she turned away in guilty silence.

"Who sent you?" Henry growled, ignoring the stab of betrayal twisting in his chest. Over the years, he experienced much heartache and disloyalty, but never did the bite sting and fester as in this moment. He shook her once more. "I command you to tell me."

When their eyes met, he saw her once enticing gaze void of all emotion. She said nothing, her lips pressed into a thin line. He released her and stepped back.

Two choices lay before him. He could drag her before Crispin and reveal her clandestine search of his chambers. This would only lead to provoking the king, who now found himself in the middle of a siege with other, more pressing issues. There would be no telling what punishments he would bring upon her for such underhanded actions.

He could detain and interrogate her himself. Knowing Crispin's temperament, this would be preferable, but should the king discover it, Henry shuddered at the possibilities such an occasion would warrant.

"If you refuse to speak, then you leave me no choice." He nodded toward her clothing. "Cover yourself."

A lesser woman would have pleaded for mercy, tearful and apologetic. But not his Ivy. *His Ivy.* The thought both pleased and disgusted him. He wanted to possess her, protect her, but could he offer his protection to a spy, a traitor? The word itself left the bite of bile in the back of his throat.

She gathered her clothes and donned them a piece at a time. Henry watched with his arms folded across his chest, blocking the door. He could not lock her in his chamber. Nay, he needed to take her somewhere no one would find her. A place he could keep her safe from Crispin.

He scowled. Nothing could save her from his wrath. She used him. Lied to him. And she would pay the penalty for her betrayal.

She laced the front of her bodice and retrieved her cap from the floor, tugging it down over her dark hair.

Henry grasped her wrist and pulled her out the door into the corridor. With measured steps, he crossed the castle, ignoring the chatter of the servants who passed. To any onlookers, they resembled a couple hellbent on finding a quiet room to spend their passions. He kept her close to him, nearly dragging her behind him as they ventured away from the occupied parts of the castle.

"Where are you taking me?" She wrenched herself from his grasp when they reached the staircase leading to the north tower.

His arm encircled her waist. "You are now at my mercy." He shoved her forward toward the tower. "Up the stairs."

Ivy stumbled when she tripped over her skirts and caught herself against the wall. She glared at him over her shoulder.

He rested his hand on his dagger. "Do not make me repeat myself."

With a huff, she spun and climbed the steps. Henry pulled a torch from the wall and followed her. He admired the way her arse swayed beneath her skirts. He wanted to push her against the stone and drive himself between her thighs. His body cared not whether she was a traitor or a spy, he wanted to fuck her until she cried out with pleasure and confessed everything to him alone.

At the top of the stairs, she opened the sturdy wooden door and entered the circular room. He closed the door behind them and twisted the key in the lock. Holding the torch aloft, he scanned the narrow space.

The tower chamber was no larger than his own, although arranged in a circle. A bed sat against the far wall, as well as a table and two chairs and a small trunk. There was no hearth for a fire, and the windows lay too high and narrow for anything but a sliver of light.

Ivy spun around to face him. "Do you intend to keep me imprisoned here?" She bared her teeth in a wicked smile. "Your whore."

Henry bristled at her words. "Tell me what I wish to know."

Ivy paced the small space. "What will you tell the queen when she requests my presence?"

"I shall tell her you have returned to your family on urgent matters." He crossed his arms and followed her movements with a critical eye.

"Are you capable of such a blatant lie?" She grinned and ran her fingertips over her lips.

"As capable as you." He arched his brow at the transformation. The once demure Ivy tugged at the strings of her bodice.

She tutted. "The loyal and honorable Henry Balmont, Duke of Westdell is incapable of lying."

"You know nothing of my capabilities." He lowered his tone in warning.

Her laugh echoed in the room, sounding like a chorus of angelic song, and yet it struck fear straight through his heart. Who was this woman?

"I will ask you once more." Henry took a measured breath. "Who sent you?"

Ivy sat on the bed. "I know not of what you speak."

Henry placed the torch in the sconce and crossed the room,

drawing to a halt just before reaching her. Fists clenched at his sides, he glared down at her.

She may look like an angel sent from heaven, but she wore the devil's smile.

"Then you will remain here." He returned her wicked grin. "I am your only ally. Should the king discover your actions, not even God himself will be able to save you."

A flash of emotion flickered in the depths of her eyes. Henry took comfort in knowing his words instilled something in her.

Refraining from stealing a punishing kiss from her cursed lips, he spun and left the tower room, taking the torch with him. He locked the door behind him, effectively sealing her inside. He tucked the key into his doublet and descended the stairs.

When he reached the bailey, he found one of the few guards he trusted training with a few of the newer knights in the ring.

"Connor." He called the knight from the edge of the ring.

The young knight joined him without hesitation. "Your grace."

"Gather your things and join me." He gestured to the castle.

Connor collected his doublet and followed Henry into the castle. He kept his silence until they reached the base of the staircase leading up into the north tower. Even from this distance, no sound could be heard from the occupant inside the tower.

"I have something of great importance which needs constant protection." Henry rested his hand on the young knight's shoulder. "I shall require you to stand guard over it."

The knight stood tall, his expression one of determination. "On my honor, I take this charge."

"I knew I could count on your diligence and discretion." He gestured to the stairs. "No one is permitted into the north tower by my order. Do you understand?"

"Aye." Connor gave a curt nod.

"I shall return once I have tended the king." Henry waved a gloved finger. "Not a soul crosses this threshold."

"None shall pass, sir. You have my vow. I will not fail you."

Connor rested his hand on the pommel of his sword strapped to his side.

"Good lad." With one last glance up the winding staircase, Henry turned his back on the knight and the mysterious Ivy locked away in the tower.

Since they returned from their journey, Henry found no peace. At every turn, he encountered an obstacle forcing him to expand his presence within the castle. Ruby and her desire to leave the castle unattended. The return of Francis from his presumed grave. And now the machinations of a female thief with whom he shared undeniable passion. Would the trials never end?

He inhaled deeply, wishing he could find a moment's respite. Since he contained Ivy within the tower and Francis remained in one of the guest chambers, Henry hoped Ruby would be content to confine herself to the immediate area. The last thing he wished for was another adventure into the forests. Who knows what kind of trouble would find him there.

The servants were milling through the corridors. He edged past them and took the stairs to the king's presence chamber. Before he could reveal Ivy's role in the theft, he needed to ascertain the value of the document she pilfered from the king's chamber.

He prayed Crispin was still abed and knocked. No answer came. He opened the door and found the room deserted. Quickly, he slipped inside and closed the door behind him.

The large ornate desk sat near the window. Henry searched the drawers and the oversized wardrobe against the far wall where many of the important documents were stored. There was no evidence of the room having been searched. Perhaps she knew exactly where to find the item.

Even more important, she had the perfect opportunity to steal it when the king was absent. Why would she put herself in this position? There were only two possibilities in his mind. Either she was a horrific thief, or she wished to be caught. But why take such a calculated risk in either case?

Henry withdrew the parchment and held it up in the

morning light. The quality of the parchment was poor, and yet the king's royal seal lay stamped upon it. He read the signature. It was not Crispin's name upon it but his father's. The letter itself was not written in English but in French.

For the first time in his life, he regretted not paying more attention to the French tutor King Edgar brought to broaden their education. As a knight, he strove to improve his physical strength and endurance. He wished now he had spent an equal amount of time expanding his mind.

He rolled the parchment and tucked it into a small pocket inside his doublet. There must be someone he could trust who was able to read French. Speaking it was one thing, but the ability to read it came damn close to impossible since most people he knew who spoke the language were illiterate. He swore beneath his breath. There was nothing here to aid in his quest.

Without delay, he removed himself from Crispin's chamber and followed the corridor to the staircase leading out into the bailey.

In his mind, he made a tally of items to retrieve for Ivy. She would freeze in the tower without sufficient clothes and blankets. Food and water.

He turned the corner and collided with someone standing in his path. All thought slipped from his mind and he bowed. "Your Majesty."

Crispin fixed him with a curious stare. "Henry. Where are you off to with such haste?"

"I have details to finalize for the festival," Henry lied.

The king's somber expression was amplified by the dark smudges beneath his eyes and a thin smile. The events of the past several days had not been kind to him. Knowing the queen's temperament, Henry could only assume Crispin and Ruby had not yet come to a peaceful alliance since he imprisoned Francis.

"We must speak. Can you tend me in my chambers?" Crispin rubbed his jaw.

"If you will beg my pardon, sire. I must attend these details post-haste, but I will tend you directly after." Henry bowed low, praying Crispin did not change his request to a command.

Crispin waved his hand in dismissal.

"My thanks, Your Majesty." Henry descended to the bailey where he located the storeroom and the supplies required for Ivy's prison cell. He could only hope Crispin found enough distraction with his brother and his wife to notice the thief in his midst.

Chapter Eleven

After the argument with Ruby, Crispin sought out the one person he counted on to help him balance the inequity in his soul. For years Henry served him as not only a knight and a companion, but a conscience of sorts. Without his guidance, he felt adrift in the darkest, coldest sea.

He scowled at Henry's retreating back. Of all mornings, he chose this one to show diligence in his duties. Crispin wanted to command him to return, to sit and aid him in uncovering the solution to this complex problem.

His commander seemed agitated and distracted. Purple bruises marred his face. Perhaps their tussle the previous night left him less than eager to discuss Francis's fate. Crispin had not intended to injure his friend, and yet the bout certainly allowed him a moment of clarity once he expended some of the rage twisting inside him.

Henry always performed this admirably well. He took Crispin's moods in stride, and when he desired to purge the demons using either fists or blades, Henry never complained, taking every strike with honor.

Yet he skirted his request this morning. Had he finally pushed his loyal companion beyond his capability by abusing his service for his own selfish needs? Crispin hung his head and flexed his hands. He could take to the pit and channel this burning need for punishment into sparring with the knights.

He could not avoid the truth or the issue at hand. Francis awaited his fate, and Ruby…he raked his hand down his face. How could he reach her? Ever since his return, she pushed him away, even though he longed for nothing more than to hold her close and treasure her. She belonged to him, body and soul. If she would only surrender herself, he could ensure her safety and happiness.

God's blood! He resisted the urge to lash out and strike something. It would do him no benefit. Both Henry and Ruby denied him, leaving him nowhere to turn except the one person who would cut straight to the heart of the issue.

His mother said little during their reunion with Francis. She watched with a predator's gaze, tracking and marking events. Waiting until the time came to speak.

Crispin inhaled, allowing his mind to settle. He traversed the short distance to his mother's solar. A maid jumped at his presence when he opened the door.

"Where is she?" he asked, searching the room.

The maid curtseyed. "She is in the village, your majesty. Preparing for the festival."

He growled in response. The poor maid squeaked before she dipped into an apologetic bow and darted out the door. He would have to seek her out. There would be no simple solutions to this confounded disaster.

With determined steps, Crispin made his way down to the bailey. Distracted by his thoughts, he nearly collided with Matthew outside the stables.

"Pardon me, Your Majesty." The gangly lad attempted to bow with an armful of weapons. A sword slipped from the pile, but Crispin caught it.

He held the sword up to the light noting the dulled blade. "I see you are sufficiently occupied."

"Aye, sire." He strained under the weight of the load. "If you will excuse me, I must deliver these to the smith."

"Carry on, lad." Crispin dismissed him, but his heart twisted with irritation. Was the whole castle averse to his company?

He scowled and walked into the village. Several guards fell into step behind him. He did not require protection, but their mere presence provided a deterrent for anyone with a complaint.

A small crowd gathered in the center of the village near the well. His attention focused on the dark red and gold cap amid the earthen tones of fabric. Colorful garlands of wheat woven with festive green and gold ribbons decorated the square. Small booths lined both sides of the streets leading into the village center.

In several days, the village would overflow with music and laughter, dancing and revelry. Every year they participated in the celebration of a plentiful harvest and the bountiful blessings of the fading summer.

In past years, Crispin spent the celebration drunk with multiple whores in his bed. Much had changed in such a short time.

The crowd parted as he neared. When he reached the center of the gathering, his mother glanced up from the children huddled around her feet.

While the children and the others bowed, Vivienne arched her brow and pressed her lips together forming a thin line. The expression bore her distaste. All words fled from his mind and whatever greeting formed on his tongue died a swift death. She was displeased with him.

Her gracious smile reappeared as she spoke to the children. "Be sure you find the best ones. Now, off with you."

The children scattered in all directions, their chatter and laughter ringing through the square, and the rest of the crowd dispersed, leaving Crispin and his mother alone. Even the guards maintained a discretionary distance.

"Mother." Crispin bowed low. When he rose, he offered his arm. "Might I have a word?"

She took his proffered arm with graceful decorum, but he sensed the undercurrent of irritation humming through her. "That depends on what words you choose." Her voice carried low between them. She smiled at those they passed while Crispin escorted her back toward the castle.

Her firm grip on his arm did not escape his notice. "Would an apology suffice?"

"Not unless you release your brother from the confines of that room." She gave him a pointed look. "Guards, Crispin? Surely you jest."

"Am I not allowed to take precautions?" He suppressed the need to justify his actions. Trust did not come easily to him, she should know this, and yet she desired him to welcome his brother with open arms.

"Against what?" She studied his profile. "I understand your hesitancy. I too harbor reservations, however, he poses no threat to you. He should be treated like a guest, not a prisoner."

Crispin scoffed. "No threat?" His voice deepened. "His presence is a threat to everything I hold dear."

"He has not come demanding the throne if that is your concern." Her words did little to soothe his fears. "Perhaps if you discuss it with the privy council, they may offer a solution that satisfies all parties."

"I dislike the idea of anyone knowing Francis is alive and well," Crispin muttered. "Such knowledge will only drive division through the kingdom."

"You believe the people will clamor for your removal and crown Francis." His mother's assessment drove a blade between his ribs nearly striking his heart.

"I believe the people will see a hero risen from the ashes. In their ignorance, they will embrace someone who has not the ability or the fortitude to rule a kingdom." Bitterness curdled the contents of his stomach. He disliked even discussing the idea of Francis claiming his birthright.

"Why should it matter? He has shown no intent to take the throne. His actions speak of a man dedicated to God. I believe he has chosen his path. It is you who fights against this invisible foe." She greeted several guards as they entered the bailey.

"Then why return at all? I will grant him leave to pursue his passion and serve God in whatever way he wishes, but in return, he must abdicate."

She withdrew from his touch. "You wish for him to go before the privy council and renounce his past and any ties to the throne." Tears shone in her eyes. "Will you also send him to some foreign land to soothe your wounded pride?"

"I will do what is necessary to protect what is mine!" Crispin's voice carried through the bailey, garnering the stares of all who occupied it.

His mother's jaw tensed. She gathered her skirts in her

hands and ignored him as she entered the castle.

Crispin swore. This was not how he envisioned the conversation. He knew his decision would not foster any love with his brother, but he never imagined it would tear the bond between him and his mother. He followed her into the dining hall.

"Mother!"

She paused in the middle of the room and spun to face him.

Crispin ignored the stares of the servants watching from the shadowed corners of the room. "Might we continue this conversation in your solar?"

Folding her hands, she regarded him for a long moment. "What makes you think this conversation is worth pursuing? It seems you have already passed your judgment on the matter."

After closing the gap between them, Crispin lowered his voice. "What would you have me do? Perhaps I do as you bid, I allow him to remain in the monastery in peace. Then one day he returns demanding the throne. Demanding his *betrothed*." His emphasis on the final word made her eyes widen. "He will not take what is *mine*."

The urge to protect Ruby overwhelmed him. Even the fleeting thought of another man coming between them enraged the already ravenous beast inside him. She may not appreciate his tactics, but at the moment, they were the only thing ensuring her complete protection.

Whether he intended to or not, Francis's return threatened everything. He would rather die fighting than willingly sacrifice his hard-won prize.

Crispin had not realized his hands were wrapped around the pommel of his sword until his mother's hand came to rest over his. His grip eased when he met her softened gaze.

"Ruby may have been his betrothed long ago, but she is your queen." Her touch soothed the chaos swirling in the pit of his stomach. "If you only ask, she will stand by your side. You must know this."

Hope tugged at the dark reaches of his soul. Instead of embracing it, he pushed it aside. After their disagreement this morning, he doubted she would come to his aid in any quarter. She may even choose to run his blade through him if given the opportunity.

Crispin wrenched himself away and glared at the lingering servants across the room. They scattered without him having to say a word.

"Have you spoken to her?" His mother's soft question made his heart twist with guilt.

"I have tried." He could not admit to anyone, especially his mother, that his bride thought him a monster incapable of mercy or understanding.

"Be patient with her. She is still learning. Both of you are. Do not say or do something you will regret." Her words of advice transformed into an ominous warning. "The future of this kingdom, your future, depends upon it."

Before he could respond, a knight appeared in the doorway. "Your Majesty, I beg your pardon. But your presence is requested in the armory."

Relief flooded him. Crispin longed for his mother's approval, but in moments such as this, he found she pushed him beyond his capacity for rational thought. She spoke out of love and honesty. A trait he admired, however, an overabundance of which drove him to madness.

He took his mother's hand and pressed a kiss to the back of it. "My apologies, Mother. Perhaps we can discuss this further once I have finished in the armory."

"I shall be finalizing the preparations for the festival taking place in four days' time." She tipped her head in acknowledgment. "Do not forget what I told you."

With a curt nod, he left her and followed the knight out into the bailey. There was much to do in preparation for the festival and the impending winter.

Francis complicated matters far beyond what he was willing to admit. It would be simple enough to slip some poison into his wine and dispose of the corpse. Even releasing him to return to the monastery and laying an ambush would suffice. He could easily lay the blame on someone other than himself.

Crispin could not kill his brother. No matter how much he allowed the dark thoughts to fester and breed in his mind, they would not take root. His mother would never forgive him for such subterfuge. If she only knew about his role in his father's death…He locked the memory in the shadows. No one would know. How could they?

When they neared the armory, Crispin nodded in greeting to the knights standing around the pit. He pretended to carefully study the men training, but his mind was distracted.

After speaking with Ruby, Henry, and his mother, he found himself no closer to a solution to his problem than when he discovered the scarred monk's true identity. Each of them granted their insight, but it mattered not. No one stood with him. How could they? They did not understand his mind, his desires.

While Ruby held his heart and Henry his conscience, his mother kept him tethered to the truth. She kept him grounded. The woman who brought him into this world could easily take him out of it should she set her mind to the task. He would be foolish to cross her.

It would be foolish to cross any of them.

Chapter Twelve

The solitude Ruby once sought so eagerly wore down her reserves. She could no longer remain silent. Even though she vowed she would not seek Crispin out, once the sun set and her maids took their leave, she slipped from her chamber into the dark hallway.

Her heart pounded in her chest. She pulled her robe tighter around her shoulders. When she reached his door, she knocked. The sound echoed through the corridor, making her wince.

Silence met her from behind the door. She lifted her fist to knock again when the bulky door opened a crack.

Handsome blue eyes met hers. *Crispin.* No matter how much he angered her, she could not stop her affection for him from claiming a piece of her heart. She longed to throw herself into his embrace and let the warmth sink into her weary soul.

Without a word, he opened the door and stepped aside, sweeping his arm wide in invitation. She crossed the threshold and entered his domain. A small voice in the back of her mind shouted in warning, but her conscience warred against it.

"I was under the impression you had no desire for my company." Crispin locked the door. "To what do I owe this unexpected *pleasure?*"

She heard the derision in his voice but elected to ignore it. His emphasis on the final word sent a shiver down her spine. "I must speak with you about an urgent matter."

"An urgent matter." Crispin poured wine into two goblets. He held one out to her in offering, which she took and cradled between her hands. "What urgent matter brings you to my chamber at this late hour?"

Ruby fidgeted with the goblet unable to meet his gaze. Her heart demanded she speak her mind and reveal the wonderful news to Crispin. But try as she might to suppress it, worry consumed her thoughts. She pinched her eyes closed and inhaled deep. His scent surrounded her.

"Come, my sweeting."

She opened her eyes to find him seated in an oversized chair beside the flames. He lay his hand on his thigh. The fabric of his tunic parted at his throat revealing his muscular chest. She longed to curl in his lap and lay her head against his beating heart.

"I promise to listen." His grin revealed a row of white teeth. A fox inviting a hare into his den. "Come sit with me."

The unease subsided as she studied his face. He lounged in the chair, arms open, his brow arched. Dark hair lay curled across his collar, contrasting with his pale skin. So regal and handsome and yet beneath that charming veneer lay unfathomable danger. The devil personified. Oh, how easy it would be to surrender to him, but at what cost?

He cocked his head. "Do you still bear me ill will?"

"I disagree with your methods." Ruby stood firm. "But I bear you no ill will."

"Yet you withdraw from my touch?" He draped his hand over the arm of the chair. "You fear me."

"'Tis your unbridled temper and relentless desire for control I fear, not you."

His gaze darkened as it slowly caressed her from head to foot. Crispin ran his tongue over his lower lip before taking a sip of his wine. Emboldened by his blatant appraisal, she set aside her wine and drew the dressing gown from her shoulders, dropping it into the empty chair beside her.

He sucked in a breath at the sight of her. In the firelight, the gown was nearly transparent. The fine fabric slid across her sensitized skin as she closed the distance between them and settled on his lap.

Crispin sat motionless, a statue hewn from flesh and bone. His warmth settled into her. She removed the goblet from his hand and drained the contents. Her gaze held his as she set it aside on the small table.

"I am not your enemy." Crispin's deep voice made her breath catch. It rumbled through her, making her unsteady. His right hand came over her thigh while the left snaked around her back, his fingertips brushing her side.

"I know." She cupped his cheek. "And I am not yours."

His eyes drifted closed at the touch. The lashes impossibly long against his skin. He pressed a kiss to her palm.

She moaned when his lips slid against her wrist. "Crispin, I must tell you—"

"I have been a fool. Forgive me." His confession effectively silenced her. It must have taken strength for him to say those simple words.

Ruby remained silent, allowing him to direct the conversation. If she spoke, it may vanish like ash on the wind. This chink in his armor exposed him, and she longed to see him uninhibited by such a cumbersome burden.

His blue eyes held hers. They drew her deep and held her suspended in an endless sea. His grip on her tightened bunching the fabric beneath his fingers and digging into her flesh.

"The thought of losing you drives all reason from my mind." He shifted her in his lap. She recognized the press of his arousal against her hip. "I will not allow him to steal you from me."

Ruby stroked his jaw. "Who?"

"My brother."

"We are bound by the law in the eyes of God." She slid her fingers over his neck and into his hair. "I belong to you and no other."

"The original agreement between Meradin and England was to unite you and Francis." His jaw clenched at the mention of his brother's name. She smoothed her thumb over the muscle. "There is still a possibility the marriage could be annulled should he choose to pursue the throne."

"But he does not wish to take the throne." She soothed him. "Nor does he have any designs on me. You have no fear on that quarter."

"There are no certainties. Until he abdicates officially in front of the council, he is a threat."

"A threat?" Ruby withdrew her hand. "Is this why you

imprisoned him?"

"He is not a prisoner," Crispin growled. "I am merely ensuring the protection of all involved."

"He is your brother, my love." She drew her fingertips along his skin. He arched into her touch. "You must be more understanding."

"I do not like the idea of him stealing what belongs to me."

"I am yours." Ruby poured her heart into his hands. "Nothing shall come between us."

He pressed his lips against hers, drawing her into a drugging kiss. "I shall possess you completely, sweeting. Your body. Your mind. Your soul. We are bound in this life and the next."

Ruby gasped against the intensity of his mouth on her skin. His hand slid beneath the fabric teasing her thighs apart. She parted for him willingly. Those talented fingers delved between her slickened folds.

He swallowed her moan with another kiss. She clung to him, unable to form a coherent thought amidst the sweet torment of his unrelenting touch.

"Perhaps I shall lock you in my chambers and have my way with you night after night until your stomach swells with my seed." He nipped at her throat and slid a finger inside her heat. "There would be no doubt then that you belong to me if you carry my child."

"Crispin." Her hands gripped his tunic as he shifted her to remove the gown. When she lay bare across his lap, her face warmed. "I already carry your child."

His mouth stilled against hers, and he drew back. Even drunk with pleasure, she saw the shock her words caused. A smile curved his lips. Joy brightened his handsome features. He rested his hand on her stomach with a sweet reverence that left her speechless.

"Mine." He kissed her hard before rising to his feet, carrying her to his bed.

She sank into the soft coverlet, dizzy with persistent ache. The need increased while she watched him draw the tunic over his head and cast it aside. His muscular body bore dark marks, not quite bruises. Where had he gotten those? They looked to be recent. Her attention shifted to his cock when he discarded his leather trews.

Crispin climbed onto the bed covering her body with his, pressing his weight into her. She wrapped her arms around his neck and welcomed him. He fit his cock to her entrance and drove deep. Her fingers dug into his shoulders and she cried out. She urged him with a thrust of her hips.

Everything faded into the distance. In this moment, there was only Crispin and her united in uninhibited pleasure. Ruby drew him closer, claiming his mouth with hers. She wanted to lose herself in the bliss only he could provide. They were bound together forever.

Crispin quickened his pace, driving his hips against hers. Pleasure spiraled upward, higher and higher until she could no longer contain it. Her climax caught hold, sending a shower of release through her body like waves crashing on the shore. She clung to him to keep from being pulled beneath the tide.

He drove into her over and over until he came with a soft curse. As though aware of his weight against her, he rolled to his side and drew her against him. She rested her head against his chest, allowing the rapid beat of his heart to lull her into contentment. The peaceful silence settled around them, leaving only the crackling of the fire in the hearth.

"Do you truly carry my child?" He smoothed his hand over her tangled hair.

Ruby propped herself up and stared down at him. "Of course."

"How long have you known?" The question seemed abrasive but his tone bore no malice.

"I suspected it for a while, but I was uncertain until the day before you returned." She tucked a lock of hair behind her ear.

"And you did not come to me the moment I returned with this news?" Lines of displeasure marred his handsome face when he frowned.

"There was not a moment of peace since your return." The distance between them grew once more.

"It should have been the first thing you told me upon my return." He sat up and folded his arms across his bare chest. "Who else knows?"

Shame flooded her. She should have told him before and now she would face his ire. "My maid, Ivy, discovered the truth. Your mother suspected it as well."

"Is that the reason you left the castle? To tell your mother of your condition?" The muscle in his jaw twitched again. She longed to reach out and caress it. Instead, she wrapped her arms around her bare chest and nodded.

"Aye. They are the only ones." Ruby held his gaze. "I have told no one else."

Crispin exhaled sharply and rubbed his hand over his face. "Why did you not come to me?"

"Because…" The shame returned and choked her, but she persisted forcing the words out. "The night before the wedding. When you and Henry…" She turned away unable to continue.

Crispin's arms wrapped around her. She sank into his embrace. "Do not concern yourself with that night, my sweet. This child is mine."

"How can you be sure?" Ruby twisted to search his face.

Crispin shrugged. "Does it matter? You belong to me, Ruby, as does this child. Nothing will challenge that."

"But—"

He covered her mouth with his, stealing her protests and allaying her fears. When they broke apart, a warmth settled through her.

"Rest, sweeting. There is much to do on the morrow." He drew her beneath the covers and held her tight against him.

Even as sleep tempted her, she could not purge the concerns swirling around in her mind. Crispin held her close, but even his presence did not chase away the demons lingering in the darkness of the unknown future before them.

Chapter Thirteen

Avoiding the king proved to be harder than Henry anticipated. He spent most of the day gathering supplies for Ivy in between meeting with the guards and soldiers in preparation for the upcoming festival. Even though this was a peaceful and joyous celebration, there must be adequate preparation for any possible problems should they arise.

Henry believed in being prepared. It served him well over the years, earning him a place beside the king. Nothing, however, could have prepared him for the woman he had locked in the north tower.

The sun set hours ago. He quietly retreated to his room and gathered the supplies in a sack. With only three days remaining until the festival, Henry knew any possibility of sleep would be forfeit.

Careful to avoid any restless occupants, Henry remained in the shadows during his short journey to the north tower. He passed a few meandering servants who seemed more interested in each other than his presence.

When he reached the tower, Connor stood exactly where he had left him earlier that day. He straightened at Henry's presence.

"Your grace." Connor bowed in respect.

"Have you spoken with anyone?" Henry asked, setting the sack on the floor beside the stairs.

"Not a soul." The young knight sagged against the wall, his exhaustion evident. "Several servants passed by, but I have seen no one else."

"Very well. Return to the barracks. Get some sleep. When the sun rises, return here." Henry issued simple instructions. The less he told the knight, the less danger he put them all in. "I shall stand watch tonight."

"Aye, sir." Without delay, Connor retreated down the corridor leading to the inner bailey.

The young knight had potential. He bore all the hallmarks of a loyal soldier. Strong, capable, and honorable. He hated to bind the young man to his secret, but he could rest knowing the lad would not break the vow he made to serve Henry without question.

Henry hefted the sack over his shoulder and climbed the stairs. By the time he reached the tower door, his breathing had become labored. Perhaps too many hearty meals and not enough training left him soft. He would need to remedy this.

He removed the key from inside the small pocket of his doublet and placed it in the lock. It turned easily and the door swung open under his hand. He braced himself for the woman inside to attack him. He deserved it, locking her in a cold tower without food or even a cloak for warmth.

She lay on the bed wrapped in a blanket asleep.

He placed the torch in the sconce and closed the door behind him being sure to lock it and hide the key on his person. As his breathing slowed, he shivered against the chill lingering in the room. There was no place for a fire, but he brought several blankets that would serve well enough to stave off the cold.

Leaving the bag by the door, he crossed the room and knelt on the edge of the bed. The blanket covered her completely. Guilt left a bitter taste in his mouth. He should have come sooner. As much as she infuriated him, he still cared for the wench.

"Ivy." He gently rested his hand on her shoulder and shook. The fabric depressed with the slightest pressure. He grasped the blanket and ripped it back revealing a formless mass of items scavenged from around the room.

Disbelief turned to rage. Where the devil was she? How had she escaped?

The cold press of steel against his throat sent a shiver of fear through him. A thousand thoughts fled his mind, leaving one simple statement of fact. She tricked him.

"On your knees." Ivy's sultry voice skated across his skin,

creating gooseflesh in its wake. "Place your hands on the bed. Slowly."

Henry followed her instructions. His head tilted, allowing him to glance over his right shoulder at Ivy. She angled the blade higher causing it to graze his throat. A stinging warmth trickled down his neck and beneath his tunic.

"I will not hesitate to slit your throat." Her warning echoed in the small room. Deep beneath the words, he sensed her indecision.

"Then do it." Henry's simple response made her inhale sharply. He prayed this decision would not be his last. "If you wished me dead, you would have already done it."

"Silence," she hissed in his ear. Her hand flexed on the hilt of the dagger she must have stolen from his belt. "Give me the key."

"Come and take it." Henry issued the challenge, hoping she would seize it.

"I will kill you and search your corpse if I must," Ivy vowed. Her sweet scent filled his head, dredging forth memories of their passion and her sweet cries of pleasure.

"Do what you must." Henry closed his eyes and braced for the inevitable, focusing on her heat behind him.

The pressure of the dagger against his throat eased enough for him to feel her hesitation. Henry seized the moment and grabbed her wrist, pulling with all his might. Ivy tumbled forward, and he spun to catch her before she collided with the bed.

"Bastard!" She fought against his hold, twisting and writhing against him.

Henry held fast to the arm wielding the dagger and squeezed until it clattered to the floor out of reach. She lashed her other hand out and clawed at his face. The sting of her nails biting his flesh made him rear back. He grabbed her other hand. She threw her weight against him. Together they tumbled to the cold floor.

Ivy landed on top of him. Even without the use of her arms, she somehow managed to straddle his waist. Her dark hair pulled free from the braid lying over her shoulder. Those enchanting eyes flared with challenge and fury. A flash of heat burst deep within him. His cock refused to take heed of the danger and hardened at the sight before him. Gone was the mild-mannered maiden replaced with a vengeful warrior goddess.

Hindered by her skirts, she struggled to keep the high ground. Henry fought back, maintaining full control of her arms, but he allowed her to remain atop him. His gaze dropped to the expanse of flesh exposed by the fraying cord of her bodice as it gaped wider with every frantic motion.

Henry licked his lips, and she stilled above him. Her heavy breaths pushed her breasts higher. He longed to take their rosy tips in his mouth. She wiggled her hips, drawing a groan from his throat when her backside rubbed against his cock.

Lust replaced the fury in her gaze. She softened against his hold and he relented, allowing her to slide lower until her hot center covered his arousal. Layers of fabric were the only thing stopping him from driving himself into her.

When she rocked her hips, Henry pulled her down and buried his hand in her hair. Their lips collided in a flurry of lips and teeth. She nipped painfully at his lower lip. He thrust his tongue in her mouth, stealing her breath for his own. The need to taste her, to devour her overwhelmed him.

She gathered her skirts around her waist. Henry freed himself, and without prompting, she slid down onto his cock. He groaned as she sank down, engulfing him in her heat. His grip on her neck tightened. She whimpered and met his thrusts eagerly.

He drove himself harder and faster. His hands settled on her hips, pinning her in place as he fucked her.

Ivy's keening cries echoed off the stone. When she found her release, the grip of her body drew out his own. He filled her, claiming her even though it went against his better judgment. This woman poisoned his mind and his soul by stealing his heart.

She collapsed against his chest, and Henry held her there. Their labored breaths chased the silence from the chamber. He wished there was a fire and a comfortable bed instead of the cold stone floor. Ivy deserved better than this. They both did.

Henry stroked a hand over her back. She curled against him and sighed.

"What is to become of us?" Ivy asked, her question revealing a vulnerability he had not anticipated.

He had no response. His loyalty lay with his king and the country of Meradin. Ivy posed a threat to both, yet he could not bring himself to expose her to the punishment she deserved. If somehow he could convince her to reveal more of her past, of who hired her, then he may be able to salvage her reputation before Crispin discovered her involvement.

"He will kill me." Ivy's statement breathed life into Henry's deepest fear. "The king will execute me for treason."

"I will not allow that." Henry stroked his fingertips along her cheek and tipped her chin so she faced him. "Tell me who sent you and your mission, and I will ensure your safety. You have my word."

Her expression softened and tears filled her eyes. She blinked them away. "You cannot save me." Her hand cupped his face. "I am worthless. Nothing can change my fate."

"You are not worthless." How could she view herself in such a way? He drew her closer wishing he could absorb her pain and suffering. "Trust me, Ivy."

"I do trust you." She shook her head and buried her face in his doublet. "But what is done is done. My course has already been set."

Confusion gripped him. "What do you mean?"

"It has begun." She shivered in his embrace. "There is no stopping it."

"I do not understand." Henry slowly climbed to his feet and carried her to the bed where he sat, drawing her against his chest. He drew a blanket around her. She leaned her head against his shoulder and pinched her eyes closed for a long breath before meeting his gaze with determination.

"Take me before the king. Reveal my actions." Conviction rang in her voice. "It is the only way to save them."

"Save who?" The skin on Henry's arms and neck pebbled

with gooseflesh. "The king and queen?"

Ivy shook her head. "The people of Meradin."

Henry had more questions than answers. Her evasiveness infuriated him, and yet he sensed she withheld information purposely to protect someone. But whom?

"Did my family send you?" he asked, piecing together the events of the wedding coinciding with his first encounter with Ivy.

"Please, do not ask more of me." She drew her lower lip between her teeth. "You must choose, Henry."

"Choose what?" His heart pounded.

"If you care for me, then you must release me." She trailed her fingers along his jaw. "If you do not, then we will both face the penalty for treason."

Guilt twisted in his gut. The truth of her words settled like a leaden ball in the pit of his stomach. How could he choose between love and loyalty? She was a thief, not a murderer. Crispin would not execute a thief, although they would both face severe punishment for their actions.

"You ask too much of me. I cannot sacrifice you." Henry held her tighter.

"Chivalrous and noble." A sad smile touched her lips. "You know nothing of my past. Of who I am."

"Then tell me," Henry pleaded. He longed to know of her family, her history. What drove her to such desperation?

"Perhaps I should. Then you would cease looking at me as though I am your moon and stars." Ivy shifted, attempting to pull away from him.

Henry captured her lips in a ravenous kiss. Heaven above, he could not get enough of her. The feel of her against him, the scent of her, the passion she ignited within him. He longed for more. For everything. But she refused to cooperate.

He kneaded her breast in his palm. She gasped against his mouth when he pulled her nipple between his fingers. He could listen to her mewling cries as she fell apart in his arms again and again. Perhaps if he seduced her enough, she would relent.

Ivy belonged to him. He claimed her without knowing

anything about her. As though his soul melded with hers, intertwining until they fused like molten steel. It was dangerous and challenged everything he represented. This glorious woman threatened his very existence, and yet he refused to retreat. She would surrender. Ivy would be his.

He made love to her again on the narrow bed. Their bodies shared heat until the rooster's crow pulled him from her warm embrace.

Nestled between the blankets, she slept as he dressed. He retrieved his dagger from the floor and tucked it into the sheath on his hip.

Henry pulled another blanket from the sack and draped it over her sleeping form. Her sweet face shone with innocence. The more he gazed at her, the less he cared who she was and where she came from. Ivy held his heart in her hands.

He would do whatever was necessary to ensure her safety, even if it meant sacrificing his own. She deserved the opportunity to set things right if only he could convince her.

Quietly, he unlocked the door and slipped from the room. Once he checked to ensure it was locked securely, he descended the stairs and waited for Connor to arrive.

The torchlight flickered against the wall. He leaned against the stone, evaluating the progression of unfolding events. There were many moving pieces on the board. Henry had always been quite adept at chess, and yet he was not nearly as proficient as Crispin.

Once Crispin knew the players, he would be able to make a move. Henry should ensure the king had all the information necessary to formulate a plan of attack. Doing so would expose the weakest pawns, and those would be sacrificed without hesitation.

Henry shivered. He could not avoid Crispin forever and this knowledge left him in torment. If he betrayed the woman he loved, would it ensure the safety of the king and queen? Come what may, he must tell Crispin or he would lose it all.

Chapter Fourteen

As much as Crispin wished he could remain abed with Ruby, there were many details left untended. Things he must address with both efficiency and expediency. He pressed a kiss to Ruby's soft lips and left her to sleep.

The servants bustled through the corridors, preparing rooms and transporting supplies. Crispin passed a half dozen before he arrived at his mother's solar. It lay empty, as did her private chamber. He wished to speak with her before attending to the monk. He pinched the bridge of his nose. His brother.

A maid passed by carrying an armful of clean linens. He stepped into her path forcing her to stop.

The young thing dipped into a low curtsey unable to meet his gaze directly. "Your Majesty." Her voice trembled.

"I am searching for the Queen Mother. Have you any idea where she may be found at this early hour?" He attempted an air of polite curiosity, but the girl seemed traumatized by the very thought of conversing with the king.

"In the kitchens, your majesty." She curtseyed again, and he allowed her to pass. Like a frightened mouse, she scurried down the hall and disappeared around the corner.

Crispin shook his head. It seemed his reputation had not improved since the coronation. Not that he minded. Fear worked quite well to motivate people to action. But he saw how the people reacted to Ruby, who showed nothing but love and concern for those around her. He pushed aside the nagging stab of guilt for his past behavior and took the servant's stairs to the kitchens.

The scent of baking bread and pastries rose through the open doorway. He peered into the room, hoping to find his mother quickly without causing any intrusion. The cook was a fearsome man who scolded Crispin many times as a lad for breaching his domain.

He spotted his mother speaking with the cook. The old man gestured wildly, his bewhiskered jowls moving faster than his hands. His mother listened patiently, her hands clasped before her. Her gaze followed the man's hands, which directed her attention to the doorway where he stood watching the exchange.

With a polite smile and a few quiet words, she extricated herself from the conversation. The cook bowed and returned to the mounds of dough on the table. His mother wove around the servants as they worked, a kind smile on her lips.

The smile disappeared when she reached the door where he stood. "I trust you slept well, my son."

"Quite well." He forced a playful grin. "Might I have a word with you in private, mother?"

Vivienne inclined her head, and Crispin stepped aside, allowing her to climb the stairs. Their presence garnered several stares from the servants who passed by. Crispin directed her toward his presence chamber, but at the last minute decided to speak with her in the small enclosed garden.

"What could you possibly have to add to your rousing declaration from yestereve?" His mother wasted no time placating his ego. She was still displeased with him and for legitimate reasons. "There is much to be done to prepare for the festival."

"Ruby is with child." Crispin cut directly to the heart of the matter. His mother's brows rose in surprise. "You knew this, and yet you did not tell me."

"It was not my place to tell you." She smoothed her hands over her bodice. "Ruby requested my silence until she could relate the good news to you herself."

Crispin crossed his arms. "Had she truly been joyous at the thought of carrying my child, she would have told me the night I returned."

"You cannot expect a new bride, ripped from all she knows and thrust into a seat of prestige, to be overjoyed at impending motherhood." The edge to his mother's voice spoke clearly of her thoughts on the matter.

"That cannot be the only reason for her silence." She knew of his indiscretion. The night before the wedding when he invited Henry into his chamber to participate in an evening of pleasure. But did Ruby reveal this to Vivienne or had she maintained her modesty by keeping the wicked secret?

"I am unaware of any other reason she would choose to keep this blessed revelation from you." She folded her hands and regarded him with a passive expression betraying nothing of her true thoughts. "But I am sure you already understand her reluctance, do you not?"

"She fears I may not be the father." Crispin stroked his jaw.

"You do not seem overly concerned about this possibility." His mother studied him closely, her vibrant gaze following his every move. "I have no desire to know what games you chose to play that night in the privacy of your chambers. However, I am concerned those actions have left Ruby uncertain as to her place in this relationship and her true value." She arched a lone brow. "Perhaps you should clarify the details for her as to remove any doubt from her mind."

"Henry and I have shared many things over the years." Crispin inclined his head slightly allowing a self-satisfied smirk to play on his lips. "But when it comes to Ruby, I am the only man she has ever known and will ever know."

"Then might I suggest you alleviate her concern about this delicate matter once and for all." Her tone softened. "If you truly love her, then tell her the truth of that night."

His mother made a valid point. The impulsive decision to include Henry that night left him imbued with a sense of power. And yet as time passed, he regretted how the guilt drove a chasm between them. He nodded in agreement.

"I shall have Ruby join you to finish preparations for the festival." He pressed a soft kiss against his mother's cheek. "My thanks for your guidance."

"Are you willing to extend the same grace to your brother?" Her question lingered heavily in the air between them.

He suppressed a growl and retreated a few steps. "That depends on how cooperative my *brother* proves to be in the matter. Good day, mother." He swept from the room without pursuing the discussion further.

As he mulled the conversation in his mind, Crispin realized his mother's concerns were founded. Try as he might, he could not avoid it. If he wished to endear Ruby to him, he would need to reveal the truth of that night. She did not deserve to harbor the guilt for his actions, even though she followed his directions. But if he spoke to Ruby, he would need to speak with Henry.

Crispin drew to a stop in the corridor near the great hall. Where in the devil was Henry? He intended to speak with him the day before, but after their initial encounter, he saw nothing of his friend for the remainder of the afternoon.

A flurry of movement drew his attention to the great hall. The servants stood on tall ladders, stringing garland between the beams and hanging the gilded royal banners. Preparations were well underway for the feast only two nights hence. In all probability, Henry was engaged in planning of his own to ensure the proper security measures were in place for the festival. With his family missing and uncertainty casting doubt in his mind, his friend would never rest until he could ensure those within the castle were protected to the fullest extent.

With determination, Crispin decided to confront his brother, the scarred monk. Surely they could come to some sort of agreement or at least an understanding. He loathed the idea of sharing anything with his brother. Miraculous as Francis's survival was, some details left Crispin uneasy.

Fortunately, he was of a gracious disposition this morning. The evening spent in Ruby's company and the wonderful news of their impending child left him in a better humor than when his brother found him two days prior. He would uncover the details of this miracle and then send his brother where no one would ever find him.

Both guards snapped to attention at Crispin's approach. He acknowledged them with a wave of his hand.

"How is our guest?" Crispin asked them.

"Not a single complaint, sire." The shorter guard replied with confidence.

"Has he had any visitors?" The question was a mere formality. He already knew the answer. There were only a handful of people who knew of the monk's presence in the castle.

"The Queen Mother comes bearing food in the morning and the evening." The other guard added without meeting Crispin's gaze.

"Very well." He opened the unlocked door. There had been no reason to lock it. Francis understood the delicacy of the situation and remained confined to his chamber.

His brother turned from where he stood gazing out the small window with a narrow view of the sky. "Your Majesty." He bowed with respect, but Crispin sensed his hesitation.

"Come now, brother. Let us not stand on formality." He gestured for his brother to sit on the bed while he took the worn chair sitting across from him.

Francis no longer attempted to hide his scarred visage. He wore it proudly, like a banner of honor. His eyes, so similar in coloring to his father's, met Crispin's with a guarded serenity.

"To what do I owe this honor." The monk interlaced his hands, hiding them beneath the folds of his robes. "I am sure you have much more pressing matters which demand your attention."

Crispin ignored the underhanded slight, intended or not. "On the contrary, your miraculous return has left a distinct impression. I remember the night we believed you lost to the flames. Our parents grieved for months. The kingdom wept at the loss of their sainted prince." It took ungodly strength to keep the sarcasm from his tainting his words.

His brother studied him for a long moment before speaking. "And you also grieved?"

"Only a heartless bastard would feel no remorse for the loss of his brother." In truth, he felt more guilt than remorse since that night, but he chose to play the part fate assigned him. "Pray, tell me, did the hand of God pluck you from the inferno?"

A smile pulled at the tight skin around Francis's mouth. "In a way, I believe He did."

"I watched the inn burn to ash. I saw the beams collapse after you ran inside. No one survived. Not the family you tried to save. Or our comrades who sought only rest and comradery after a long day of training. All of them gone in an instant. Had we not been delayed, we also would have been trapped and killed." Crispin slowly lost his patience. "How in the devil did you survive?"

"The moment I entered the inn, I knew it was too late. I could not save them." Francis's voice softened, but his gaze held Crispin's fast. "The doorway caved in. I followed the shouts and found Simon and Timothy hiding. They pulled me down into the cellar. The roof collapsed. We were engulfed in flames."

Crispin listened to the tale with rapt attention searching for any hint of deception. He remembered the night clearly, although he never imagined the horror of being trapped in the heart of the blaze.

"We extinguished the flames, but the damage was already done." Francis gestured to his face. "I remember very little after that. Simon's voice. A tunnel. The excruciating pain. Shouting and then darkness."

"A tunnel." Crispin grasped the detail without hesitation. "Beneath the inn?"

"Aye." Francis inhaled deeply. "Simon knew of it. The innkeeper used it to smuggle supplies."

"What became of Simon and Timothy?" This new information changed his perspective on the events of that night. "Did they also survive?"

"They both perished at the monastery from their injuries. Burned as I was, nearly beyond recognition, I should have joined them." Francis crossed himself. "May the Lord have mercy on their souls. I know not how or why I was spared the same fate."

"How did you reach the monastery with such grievous injuries?" His mind spun with possibilities, trying to reconstruct the story his brother told. It could very well be possible, but what proof did he have to verify his outrageous claim?

"The tunnel entrance lay in the forest behind the monastery. Several monks were loading a wagon when they spied movement in the brush and found us."

"How fortunate for you." The snide comment spilled from his lips.

"But not for the two men who saved my life." Francis inclined his head and frowned. "There are days I wish the Lord had taken me along with my brothers-in-arms. Every day, I wake in persistent pain. I shall never again garner the smiles and favors of lovely maidens as I ride through the village. In being blessed with a second chance at life, I must embrace this cursed form." He took a deep breath. "The Lord works in mysterious ways, brother. I have chosen to follow where He leads and be thankful in all things for His mercy."

"Then why are you here?" Crispin hid the effect of his brother's words on his conscience. In truth, Francis bore nearly no resemblance to the man he once knew. Were it not for his eyes and the confirmation of his words, he would be unrecognizable as the heir to the throne.

"When Henry discovered me, I knew I could no longer hide in the shadows. Mother deserved to know the truth." The simplicity of his statement revealed the honesty of his soul.

"And what of Ruby?" A protective fury rose from his impatience. "Have you lured her into your confidence over the years?"

"Quite the opposite." Francis chuckled. "Our acquaintance is based on a mutual arrangement. She delivered medicines for the monastery on behalf of her mother, and in return, I offered a place of refuge should she seek it."

"You have no design on her?" He refrained from clenching his hands into fists.

"Ruby is a beautiful and desirable woman." Francis's words intensified Crispin's fury. "But I am incapable of enjoying the company of a woman."

The confession brought Crispin's thoughts to a standstill. "You are incapable or disinterested?"

"The damage caused by the fire extends well beyond my physical appearance." Sadness filled Francis's eyes. "I am unable to engage in intimate relations with a woman. My ability to provide an heir was stolen by my extensive injuries."

A perverse sense of relief filled Crispin. His brother could not continue the line of succession. His admission clearly revealed his inability to take the throne.

"There is no cause for concern. Ruby is yours, and I will not come between what God has ordained." Peace settled around them. "May God grant you every happiness, Crispin."

"Why did you not come forward?" Crispin asked the question again, hoping for a more honest answer.

"By the time I recovered, the kingdom believed me dead. And so I was." Francis closed his eyes for a moment as though coming to acceptance with his decision once more. "I chose to remain in the shadows and allow the kingdom to continue without the promise of my ascent to the throne because I was no longer physically able to fulfill the duties expected of me."

"And you still feel this way?" Crispin leaned forward, bracing his arms on his thighs.

Francis glanced out the window. "My fate lies upon a different path."

Ignoring his brother's cryptic response, Crispin pressed forward. "On the morrow, I will bring you before the privy council. If you truly believe as you state, then you can formally abdicate the throne and I will leave you in peace to live out your days as you so choose."

"I shall pray and fast until then." Francis rose and bowed. "May God grant you mercy."

"And you, brother." Crispin stood and clasped his hand on his brother's shoulder. Francis stilled at the touch but not before his dark gaze fixed on Crispin.

Feeling lighter than he had in weeks, he retreated from the small chamber and left his brother to his prayers. Crispin allowed himself a grin. This information played perfectly into his plans. Francis was no longer a threat to the throne. Nor could he touch Ruby.

A weight lifted from his shoulders. He would prepare to meet with the privy council. Francis would abdicate, and they could put the entire affair behind them before the festival officially began. He could then send his brother far away where he could serve God in whatever manner he saw fit.

Meradin would be his without question or challenge.

He would seek out Henry and relay this new information. There was much to be done and very little time in which to complete it. One final obstacle to overcome and everything would be right in his kingdom.

Chapter Fifteen

Ivy had disappeared. When young Mina arrived alone to help her dress, Ruby found the absence of the maid concerning. For the past two months, she served quite faithfully always able to anticipate her mistress' desires. Ivy and Mina were a comfort to Ruby.

"Where is Ivy?" she asked Mina who gathered a gown from the wardrobe, dragging the hem on the ground because of her diminutive stature. Poor lass served quite well, although being so young left her inadequate in some tasks.

"I have not seen her in two days, your majesty." Mina's delicate voice trembled.

"Where did you see her last?" Ruby attempted to piece together the missing maid's whereabouts. "Perhaps someone else has seen her."

Mina remained silent as she helped Ruby don the green gown with gold embroidery. Ruby studied the girl. Her gaze downcast, lips pinned firmly together. Even her hands trembled.

"My dear. I asked you a question." She abhorred using such an abrasive tone, but the girl knew something and from the hesitancy in her expression, she was not about to reveal it of her own free will. Her stern command filled Mina's eyes with tears.

"Please do not be upset." Mina sobbed. "I should have been abed as you directed, but I could not sleep and went to speak with one of the kitchen maids as we are the same age." Her chatter blurred together as the confession spilled forth. "When I attempted to return to the chamber I share with Ivy, I saw her with a man."

Ruby's brow arched. A man? How interesting. It did not surprise her in the slightest. Ivy was a lovely woman with curves and charm enough to attract any knight in the castle.

"Which man?" she pressed as the possibilities unfolded in

her mind.

"A handsome knight." Mina nodded quickly, her eyes wide and dreamy, tears forgotten.

"Does this handsome knight have a name?" Ruby suppressed a chuckle at the girl's assessment.

"Of course, your majesty." Her cheeks turned a dark shade of pink. "The king's right hand, His Grace, Henry Balmont, Duke of Westdell."

Ruby's grip on the laces of her gown slipped. She quickly fastened them in a loose knot and knelt to face Mina. "You saw Ivy with Henry two nights ago. Are you quite certain?"

Mina nodded. "Oh, yes, ma'am. I saw him kiss her and then he led her toward his quarters."

At least they had the decorum to take their amorous encounters to a more private location. Her face heated at the thought of this child being exposed to such a display.

Ruby cleared her throat. "From this day forward, you are to remain in your chambers once I dismiss you for the night, is that understood?"

"As you wish, my queen. Although, it matters very little. I know what happens between a man and a woman." Mina's gaze dropped as the blush deepened.

She cupped the girl's chin in her hand. "That may well be, but you are still young and I would rather ensure your protection while you are in my care."

"Grammercy, your majesty." Mina dipped into a deep curtsey.

"Are you able to plait my hair?" Ruby rose and crossed to where the chair sat by the fire.

"I have watched Ivy closely." Mina's face blossomed into a joyful grin.

While Mina braided Ruby's hair, her excitement for the upcoming festivities bubbled to the surface. She chattered on about the delicious pastries in the village and the games. The details she shared from prior years gave Ruby a reprieve from her concerns. Immersed in the girl's excitement she found herself drawn into the anticipation.

After the tension of the past few days, she embraced the levity of such a simple exchange. The monk, Ivy, and Crispin were pushed to the back of her mind. Mina shared her favorite stories of the festival.

Vendors and guests from across the kingdom would arrive over the next day in preparation for the festivities. Mina confessed her desire to see the bonfire in the square since her mother never allowed her to attend before.

Once Mina finished her braid, Ruby pinned it beneath a simple sheer netting. She hated covering her head with anything other than a hood.

"Is there anything else, my queen?" Mina gathered her discarded nightgown in her arms.

"Go to the kitchens and see if they require help preparing for the feast." Ruby dismissed the girl. No matter how much she wished to give her the afternoon to explore the village, she would have the following day to do so. There was much work to be done.

Ruby spent enough time locked away, avoiding her duties. She took a deep breath and decided to seek out Vivienne. Her unfounded fears concerning Crispin's response to her news disappeared after their conversation.

If anything, it brought them to a closer understanding. Crispin, while still the same selfish cur he was before, seemed to transform in small increments. He vexed her. Infuriated her. Confounded her. And yet she loved him. He may not be a saint. His tongue as wicked as it was sinful. But he cared deeply for her, of that she was certain.

The servants bustled through the castle, cleaning and decorating. Ruby gasped in delight when she stepped into the dining hall. Sunlight streamed through the windows along the eastern wall. The banners glistened against the stone. Garlands hung from the exposed beams overhead. The tables bore wreath-draped candelabras.

"I think it could use more color." Vivienne came up beside her interrupting her peaceful admiration of the space. "It is good to see you have much recovered."

"Aye." Ruby studied the banner in the distance, unable to meet her gaze. "My thanks for your understanding."

Vivienne inclined her head with a graceful tilt of acknowledgment. "I take it you have spoken to Crispin."

"He is aware of my condition," Ruby confirmed her face heating at the memory of his reaction.

"And is it as you feared?" she asked, taking Ruby's arm and leading her toward the arched doorway.

"Quite the contrary." She smiled, feeling lighter than she had in a long time. "He is overjoyed at the prospect of becoming a father."

"As he should be." Vivienne squeezed her arm lovingly. Side-by-side they stepped into the inner bailey.

The shouts of sparring knights mingled with the clanging of the smith's hammer striking the anvil. Chickens scattered as they pressed onward. Maids carried baskets of produce toward the kitchens while stealing glances at the guards lining the training ring and chattering amongst themselves.

Ruby scanned the men, trying not to look too obvious in her quest to find the one she wished to speak with.

"If you seek Crispin, he is tending to our distinguished guest." Her cryptic description deterred curious servants should they pass by and overhear their conversation.

"I wished to speak with Henry." Ruby lowered her voice. "One of my maids is missing, and I have reason to believe he was the last person to see her."

Vivienne's brow arched in surprise. "Henry takes his duties quite seriously. Crispin's unfortunate habits have influenced the poor boy for years. It would be good for him to find a suitable bride and save the reputations of the unfortunate girls employed in the castle."

"He deserves the love of a good woman, no matter what family she comes from," Ruby agreed before redirecting the conversation to the remaining preparations for the festival.

A cluster of guards fell into step behind them as Ruby and Vivienne reached the gate leading to the village. The gently sloping hill dipped into the village already blossoming with activity. From the short distance, she could make out the colorful banners lining the streets.

"The vendors will be arriving this afternoon to prepare the market. On the morrow, guests will arrive from around the kingdom. We shall have a feast in the evening and revelry through the night. The following day will be games and festivities for the children while their parents sell their goods in the market." Vivienne beamed with pride overlooking the village.

She poured so much love and attention into this festival. Vivienne worked tirelessly to ensure the people of Meradin were considered in every aspect. She truly was a queen of the people. Ruby desired nothing more than to strive to live up to her standard.

They returned to the sanctuary of the inner bailey and the gates closed securely behind them. Ruby cringed at the immediate pressure of being caged. She inhaled deeply in an attempt to chase away the tension from her mind.

"Ah, here comes Henry now." Vivienne released her arm. "I shall give you a moment to speak with him. Seek me out in the kitchens when you have finished your discussion."

Henry strode across the bailey, his attention shifting over his shoulder.

"Your grace," Ruby called out.

His piercing gaze snapped up, meeting hers. He swept into a low bow as she approached. "My queen. How may I be of service?"

"Walk with me a moment." She straightened when he fell into step beside her.

His body remained tense. He scanned all who passed by.

"Are you well, Henry?" Ruby asked, her voice low between them.

"Of course, ma'am." He redirected his attention to her. "Why do you ask?"

"You seem distracted." She pressed gently not wanting to cross a line in showing her concern. With their complicated history, it did not matter. They were much closer than many would surmise upon first glance. Ruby trusted him with her life, could he not trust her with his concerns?

"My apologies, my queen." Henry offered a small smile.

"I have heard a rumor about you, Henry."

He tripped over his feet but recovered quickly. "A rumor?" He laughed, but it sounded forced.

"I have heard you have taken an interest in my ladies' maid." She glanced at him gauging his reaction. "Ivy. Lovely girl, long chestnut hair, deep green eyes, buxom."

A blush stole across Henry's cheeks. "She is lovely, I do confess."

"Have you stolen her away and hidden her somewhere?" Ruby teased, enjoying his discomfort at the conversation.

All the color drained from Henry's face. He drew to a stop. "Why would you accuse me of such a thing?"

Ruby stopped and faced him. "You could keep her for yourself and have your wicked way with her without interruption."

He closed his eyes and shook his head. "Would you truly think me capable of such a thing, my queen?"

"I jest with you, Henry." She shoved his arm playfully. "I have not seen her in two days, and I grew concerned. One of the other servants saw you together, I hoped you may know where I may find her. I confess, I am in desperate need of her assistance. These intricate garments are more witchcraft than fashion." His silence made her frown. "Do you know where she is?"

Henry met her gaze steadily. "'Tis true. Ivy and I shared a night in each other's company. She left me early the following morning and I have not seen her since."

Disappointment filled her. "And she did not mention where she was going or when she would return?"

"Her family." He shrugged. "Her mother was ill and she needed to tend her."

Ruby studied him closely. Henry bore the stoic expression of a true courtier, but she sensed there was more beneath the surface. He knew more than he was prepared to reveal of that she was certain. If she pressed him further, he would hide his obvious attraction to the maid.

"I do hope she returns before the festival." Ruby pouted, playing the role of disinterest in their relationship and focusing solely on the swift return of her maid. "I admit to being quite inept when it comes to the styles of court. Ivy seems to know exactly what I need before I do."

Henry's jaw clenched before he replied. "I am sure she will return soon, my queen." He bowed. "If you will pardon me, I must attend my guards."

"Very well. My thanks for your help, Henry." Ruby watched him cross the yard. His tall figure cut a striking image against the crowd gathering around him.

Henry Balmont, loyal servant and peer of the realm, lied to her. He knew exactly where Ivy was. Why he kept this from her, she knew not. But at some point, he would reveal it, whether he intended to do so or not.

Ruby might be the Queen of Meradin, but she was still the Lady of the Forest deep in her soul. Those rogue skills did not vanish in her short duration as queen.

Formulating a plan, Ruby made her way into the heart of the castle where Vivienne worked in the kitchens.

Mina waved from the corner where she peeled vegetables with another young girl. She pulled them both aside and gave them both specific instructions. With a promise of a special surprise, the two girls bounded off up the stairs.

With a sly smile, Ruby joined Vivienne, who spoke with a small band of servants. She could hardly focus on the task at hand.

Henry and his secrets would come to light, of that she was sure.

Chapter Sixteen

After his conversation with Ruby in the bailey, Henry found himself even more distracted. He attempted to avoid Crispin's presence, but it was impossible to avoid both the king and queen when enclosed in such close quarters.

He channeled the frustration coursing through him into several bouts in the lists. Combat eased his conscience, at least in the moment. Round after round, he poured his energy into training the young knights. When his arms ached from holding the sword and sweat soaked through his tunic, he relented.

As he stepped from the yard, he spied a group of maids watching from the shade cast by the walkway encircling the castle wall. They watched the group of men training with rapturous attention. Henry retrieved his doublet and dagger before retreating into the castle.

His small chamber suited his purposes, although he wished there was space enough for a wooden tub. His newly appointed position earned him a more prestigious chamber, should he desire to move, as well as access to whatever he deemed necessary in pursuit of his duties. Which at this moment, he desired nothing more than a bath.

Once he located a servant who was able to obtain the washtub as well as the water, Henry took a few moments to sneak into the kitchen and pilfer a bowl full of dried meats and cheeses, some apples, and a half loaf of bread.

When he returned to his room, he found the tub already half-full of steaming water. Several servants carried buckets into the room and poured them into the tub while he sat on the bed nibbling on a delicious apple.

The servants left him in peace after they finished. Henry stripped off his clothes and sank into the inviting heat of the bath. He leaned his head back against the rim of the tub and closed his eyes. The tension slowly eased from his shoulders and back.

His mind wandered to his conversation with Ruby earlier. She could not possibly know his part in Ivy's sudden disappearance. Her teasing remarks left him shaken. Had she truly known, she would have cornered him and pried the truth from his lips on pain of death.

Ruby might be the Queen of Meradin, but she was a force to be reckoned with when she confronted injustice. Guilt rankled him. His actions toward Ivy had been less than honorable, but was his duty not to protect the king and queen? To ensure the protection of the kingdom?

He dipped beneath the water and washed the grit from his hair. The pungent scent of the soap lingered on his skin. Try as he might, he could not wash away the guilt staining his soul. Ruby would see through his lies.

After darkness fell, he would move Ivy. For her safety as much as his own. She hid the truth from him, even though she revealed glimpses of her heart in their tender moments. Fear held her captive. How could such a woman have any fear? She threw herself into the lion's den, daring to challenge Crispin's wrath should she be discovered. Even when he locked her away in the tower, she resisted his inquiries. She attacked him and attempted escape, though it may cost her life. But when he pleaded for the name of the man who sent her, fear reflected in her beautiful eyes.

"Fuck!" He slammed his fist against the water and splashed it over the sides of the tub.

There could be no other course of action. He must move her. But where? Henry pinched the bridge of his nose. He had very little connection to anyone living outside the castle walls. It would need to be close enough for him to return before dawn and secure enough to protect his prize.

Damn it to hell. He would need to think on it. There was naught he could do until after dark. He would ensure Crispin and Ruby were both adequately distracted before attempting to move Ivy, but he needed to speak with his prisoner before then. One last opportunity to reveal the information she so diligently withheld.

Henry rose from the now tepid water and dried himself with a clean cloth. He donned fresh clothes and ran his fingers through his hair. At least he no longer smelled like an overworked draft horse.

Perhaps he should seek out Crispin before he attended Ivy. It would be better to ensure the king's attention remained focused on something other than his own activities. He could also ascertain what Crispin intended to do about his brother. They could not keep him confined to his chamber in the castle indefinitely.

He wrapped the remaining food in a small sack and tucked it into the chest at the foot of his bed. Once he spoke with Crispin, he would retrieve it. Ivy must be starving. He would pinch a pitcher of wine from the cellar after he spoke to the king.

When Henry stepped into the hallway, a flash of movement at the end of the corridor caught his eye. He wandered in the direction, hoping it was one of the servants who brought up his bath. But when he reached the corner, he found the queen's young maid struggling to lift the latch on the door leading down to the great hall.

"Mina, is it?" He reached out and lifted the latch.

"Yes, your grace." She turned and bobbed a small curtsey. Her gaze remained fixed on the floor.

"Would you fetch some servants to remove the bath from my chamber?" he asked, searching her with curiosity. What reason would she have to be in the knight's wing?

"Of course, sir." Before he could stop her, she quickly slipped through the doorway and down the staircase.

What an odd young girl. He would ask Ruby about her later. As much as he trusted his men to adhere to his standards and a strict moral code, having such a temptation in their midst could lead to trouble in the future. Mina still looked like a child, but Henry glimpsed the beautiful woman she would become lurking beneath the surface. It would only be a matter of time before she drew the attention of the men inside the castle. It was his duty to protect those in his care.

He pushed aside thoughts of Ivy, Mina, and Ruby. During the short walk to Crispin's presence chamber, Henry refocused his mind on the tasks placed upon him.

Outside the king's door, he straightened his doublet and smoothed his hand over the fabric. With a deep breath, he knocked on the ornate door before opening it.

Crispin glanced up from where he sat behind his desk. He rolled the parchment he had been reading and set it aside.

"Where in the devil have you been hiding?" He rose from his seat and circled to meet Henry on equal footing.

"I spent the day training and finalizing plans to ensure the festival is secure." Henry bowed in an attempt to avoid his friend's penetrating gaze.

"You have been avoiding me." Crispin leaned against the desk and gripped the edge with both hands. "I had hoped to find you bedding some smitten maiden, keeping her well sated in your chamber."

Henry nearly flinched at the assessment. Such a comment was not unlike Crispin, and yet the arrow struck too close to the center of its intended target. "I regret to disappoint you, my liege. There were many details concerning the festival which I found needed my attention."

Crispin cocked his head, studying his companion with a keen eye. Henry hated how observant he could be when he put his mind to it. He steeled himself against the urge to make a hasty retreat and instead focused the conversation elsewhere.

"The festival begins upon the morrow's eve with the harvest feast. I have ensured every soldier and guard will be posted around the village as well as the castle during the celebration." Henry relaxed as he explained his plans in detail.

As he spoke, Crispin listened, asking questions and requesting clarification on several points before nodding. "Very well. It seems as though you have this well in hand, as I knew you would."

"What of Francis?" Henry asked the one question he feared might cast a shadow over his friend.

A wicked grin crossed his friend's lips and he shrugged. "I spoke with him this morn. He is of no threat to me or the throne."

"Has he agreed to meet with the privy council and formally abdicate?" Relief flooded Henry. While he always thought Francis would make a better leader than Crispin, he had been absent for so long and so altered by the events of that night, Henry feared he would be unable to rule as he once would have.

"He will have no choice. If what he revealed during our conversation this morning is brought to the attention of the privy council, he will be required to abdicate the throne." Crispin's triumphant expression chased away any concerns lingering in Henry's mind.

"What did he reveal?" Henry leaned closer.

"The fire rendered him impotent. He is unable to sire children and therefore incapable of perpetuating the royal bloodline." Crispin practically glowed at the knowledge. "Once I reveal this to the privy council, along with my own revelation, the legitimacy of his claim to the throne will undoubtedly be cast asunder."

"What revelation?" Even though he asked the question, Henry already knew the answer.

"Ruby is with child." Crispin's gaze narrowed, his eyes blazing like blue flames. "*My* child."

The confidence of his statement banished the doubt which hovered over Henry since Ivy revealed the news two nights prior. The events of that night remain blurred and distant in his mind like a dream lost in the thick fog. Flashes of memory rose in his mind's eye, but he could not tell whether they were real or just figments of his drink-addled head.

"This is wonderful news, your majesty." Henry cleared his throat.

"I intend to make a formal announcement at the feast."

"What of Francis?" The outlying uncertainty nagged at Henry. They could not celebrate as a kingdom with his brother trapped in a cell.

"We meet with the privy council on the morrow just before

midday. Once Francis reveals himself and his intention to abdicate, then he can go on his merry way." Crispin rose to his full height and clasped Henry on the shoulder. "What ails you? You look quite solemn."

"Forgive me, sire." Henry paced the length of the room, stopping to gaze out the window overlooking the bailey. Darkness settled outside masking the occupants in flickering shadows cast by torches around the yard. "It may be nothing, but I feel as though there may be something greater at play here."

"Have you any proof?" Crispin came alongside him.

Ivy. Her name sat on the tip of his tongue, but he could not betray her. Not when he cared so deeply for her. It only reaffirmed his need to draw a confession from her before the morning and send her away.

"Nothing but a worrisome nagging in the pit of my stomach," Henry admitted with regret.

"I value your abilities as a soldier as well as your counsel as my closest companion, but your intuition has been wrong before." Crispin chuckled. "Remember when you told me you thought Simon and Timothy were plotting treason when you caught them talking with that old washerwoman. Or the time you were convinced that Francis purposely let you fall into that mudhole."

Henry had no proof to the contrary of those statements, not that it mattered. They were silly accusations lost to time and the deaths of their comrades. He let them fall to the wayside and nodded. "Forgive me, sire. 'Tis my responsibility to ensure the safety of all in my care. You can understand my overabundance of caution on the matter, surely?"

"None can surpass your skill, Henry. 'Tis one of the many reasons I keep you by my side as my right hand." His overconfident façade dropped for a moment revealing the true Crispin beneath all the pomp and pride. "I trust you with my life."

A lump formed in Henry's throat. He forced it down and replied with a single nod.

"I must finish some preparations for the meeting with the

privy council." Crispin returned to his desk. "Find a willing wench and sate yourself, my friend. You have earned some rest."

"My thanks, sire." He left Crispin to his parchments. Once the door closed between them, Henry slumped against it. The conversation had gone better than he had anticipated, but uncertainty coiled in his gut. Plans were in motion, he could feel it, and yet the only evidence he held lay in the north tower.

Henry made his way to the wine cellar and filled a wineskin. Then he returned to his chambers and retrieved the food he had hidden earlier. The tub had been removed in his absence. The scent of soap and leather mingled in the air.

Tucking the pilfered items into a bag, he pushed away the guilt of lying to Crispin and Ruby. He would not dwell on it. Instead, he would get Ivy to confess and then send her away, somewhere she would be safe.

When he crossed the castle, laughter and conversation from the great hall echoed down the corridors. Every knight and servant would be occupied with the evening meal. He used this time to slip undetected into the narrow passageway leading to the north tower.

Connor sat at the base of the steps. The knight followed instructions perfectly, keeping his assignment silent from the other men. He rose to his feet quickly when he saw Henry approach.

"Anything to report?" he asked the knight.

"Nothing, your grace." Connor bowed his head.

"Very well. You are relieved for the night." Henry rested his hand on the young man's shoulder. "Remember. Speak not a word of this."

"You have my vow of honor." The conviction of the man's words resonated in Henry's soul.

"Go. Enjoy your evening. Get some rest. On the morrow, we have much to attend."

Connor took his leave. Once he vanished from sight, Henry climbed the stairs to the tower. He unlocked the door and opened it with caution.

"Ivy?" he called out softly, entering the room and lifting the torch high.

She sat on the bed bundled beneath the blankets. "H-here." Her teeth chattered.

A stab of conscience pierced his heart. With no fire and the evenings growing colder, this small room offered little reprieve from the chill.

Henry closed and locked the door before joining her on the bed. He gathered her in his arms, allowing his heat to warm her. She snatched the bag from where he sat it on the bed and retrieved the meager fare from inside.

He watched silently as she stuffed the meat and cheese into her mouth. When she tore pieces of the bread off with her teeth, she looked almost feral. His heart twisted.

She opened the wine and took a drink. A small dribble escaped the corner of her mouth. Henry wiped it away with his thumb.

"I can send you far from here. Somewhere safe and hidden. No one will find you." Henry cupped her cheek. "Tell me who sent you."

Fear flashed in her eyes replaced quickly by irritation. "Must you persist? I told you before, I cannot."

"If you do not, I will be forced to take you before the king." He hated the helplessness churning in his conscience. "Would you rather face his punishment?"

"Aye. Without question." Ivy's eyes glinted in the torchlight.

"Damn stubborn woman," Henry swore but held her close.

A knock at the door made his heart cease beating. He and Ivy exchanged a fearful glance before Henry rose from the bed being sure to tuck her out of sight on the bed beneath the blankets.

He unlocked the door and opened it a crack. Surely the torchlight played tricks with his sight. His heart sank like a stone into the depths of Skye Lake. Visions of his execution danced in the back of his mind. His secret had been found out.

Ruby stood at the top of the winding staircase, her brow furrowed and lips pursed. She crossed her arms. "Allow me entrance, Henry, or I shall summon the king."

Chapter Seventeen

Torn between fury and relief, Ruby braced her hand on the door. The torchlight flickered across Henry's face. His jaw clenched at the sight of her. She saw similar guilty expressions painted on thieves caught with their pockets full of stolen coin.

A flash of movement drew her attention to the dark space beyond the stunned knight. The familiar friendly face of her maid materialized beside him. Her eyes held the same uncertainty as Henry's.

"Ivy." Fury overtook reason, and she rounded on Henry. "What is the meaning of this?"

Resigned, Henry stepped aside, admitting her to the small tower chamber. He locked the door behind her and motioned toward the chair. "Please, sit."

Ruby shook her head. "I asked a question, sir. I demand an answer."

Henry paced the length of the room running his hand through his hair. When he finally stopped and faced her, the resignation scrawled across his handsome features tore at her heartstrings.

"Two nights ago, I…I discovered Ivy in possession of a piece of parchment she procured from the king's presence chamber." He met Ivy's gaze. Ruby saw the intensity of the exchange, but could not focus on the amorous relationship because the implications of his statement put them both at risk.

"You are a thief?" She turned to Ivy and scowled before returning her attention to Henry. "Why did you not bring this to the king?"

Henry scoffed. "Do you think Crispin would show mercy to anyone caught stealing from him? He would have her labeled a traitor and sentenced accordingly."

Her heart softened. Henry must truly love her if he put

himself between her and his longstanding commitment to the king. His blood ran thick with honor and loyalty. For him to threaten such a strong moral obligation spoke clearly of his devotion to this woman. Ruby relaxed, dropping her hands to her sides.

"Who sent you?" Ruby directed the question to Ivy, but Henry responded.

"She refuses to reveal this information." Henry straightened. "This is why I have kept her confined to the tower. I have attempted to draw the name from her lips myself in the hopes of avoiding any unpleasant repercussions from the king."

Ivy remained stoic, her chin tilted up in defiance and pride, but her lips pursed tightly. She reminded Ruby very much of herself. That resonating bond secured her decision. Her focus on Ivy never wavered.

"Leave us." Her strength echoed in her tone. "I wish to speak with your *prisoner* alone."

"My queen, I cannot—"

"Immediately." She practically growled the word without removing her gaze from Ivy's.

Henry snapped to attention and retreated from the chamber, slamming the door with enough force to make the stone walls tremble. Once the lock slid into place, Ivy visibly relaxed. Her body trembled as she dropped onto the edge of the bed and hung her head in her hands.

"Please forgive me, Your Majesty." She sobbed, her face hidden from view.

"Enough, Ivy." Ruby approached the maid but did not reach for her in comfort. "Save your tears for Henry. There shall be no more lies between us."

Silence descended as the sobbing ceased. Ivy dropped her hands to her lap and lifted her gaze. Remnants of tears shimmered against her pale cheeks, but those green eyes held no remorse.

"I do not care what tale of woe you fed Henry. 'Tis obvious he is smitten with you." Ruby pulled the chair closer and sat down across from the maid she once trusted. "Though I cannot blame him. You had me quite convinced of your loyalty."

"Men are always easier to convince," Ivy admitted with a small smile.

"Especially when plied with sweet kisses and hours of pleasure." Ruby agreed, remembering the piece of advice her mother once shared with her what felt like a lifetime ago. "Sex can be a powerful motivator."

Ivy smirked at the observation

"Who are you?" Ruby continued, undeterred by the challenge. She was determined to unravel the mystery of Ivy's actions as well as her origins should it take an act of God.

"A humble tool," Ivy replied simply.

"Who sent you?"

"A man."

"Come now. If you wish me to plead for mercy on your behalf, I will need more than the petulant responses of a child." Ruby cheered inwardly as the gloating grin disappeared from Ivy's lips. "Tell me who sent you."

"I do not know their name," Ivy confessed with a shrug.

"So you are a thief for hire with no allegiances."

"A thief. A spy. An assassin. I do whatever is required of me." Ivy leaned closer. "But my services are not for hire."

"You have no allegiance? No king? No commander?" Ruby studied her expression carefully for any sign of deceit. "If your services are not for hire, then you are beholden to this man."

Ivy gave the slightest nod. Had Ruby not been watching her, she would have missed it.

"I know nothing of your past or your heart, Ivy." Desperate to reach beyond the barrier erected between them, Ruby offered a token of sincerity. "But should you wish to change your circumstances, I am willing to listen and offer my aid."

"This is far beyond your reach." Ivy's bravado faded, giving a glimpse of the vulnerability beneath the surface of her tough exterior. "I must see this through until the end."

"The end?" Fear seized Ruby's heart. "You were not merely sent to retrieve a slip of parchment, were you?"

Ivy did not respond, but her gaze shifted away from Ruby's.

Using every fiber of patience she possessed, Ruby pressed onward and refrained from taking a blade to the woman's throat and demanding a confession.

"What is your mission?" she asked, terrified of what the answer might be.

Ivy lifted her gaze and sighed. "Wait for the signal."

"What signal?" Ruby grew frustrated with the vague replies.

"I know not. The message said I would know when it was revealed." The confusing replies did nothing to ease Ruby's conscience. What kind of person gives such vague instructions?

"Were you sent to kill the king?" Ruby opted for the more direct approach.

Ivy chuckled. "If I were, he would already be dead."

"So you were not sent to kill." Relief filled her at Ivy's affirming nod. "So you lie in wait, spying on us as we go about our lives until you receive a signal."

"Aye."

"And after you gather details of our lives and daily routines, what do you do with this information?"

Ivy pondered the question for a long moment. "Nothing."

Ruby's patience snapped. "I grow weary of your evasions and lies, Ivy. Tell me what I wish to know, or so help me God, I will drag you before the king this moment and let him take your head." Righteous indignation burned through her. She rested her hand on the dagger hidden beneath her skirts. "Speak, now."

The maid's eyes narrowed, searching and holding Ruby's gaze fast. They remained locked in silent battle until Ivy relented with a heavy exhale.

"There is a cove in the forest. I place my notes there for the messenger to deliver them."

Ruby relaxed and settled back against the chair. "You have never met the messenger nor the man who gives you direction?"

"Never."

The longer she spoke with Ivy, the more she realized the complexity of the situation. Ivy seemed unrepentant for her actions, however, Ruby could see the woman was not wholly without a conscience. Perhaps she could use this to her advantage. Her gaze raked over the maid she once trusted. Dare she place her faith in such a person when it seemed perfectly obvious they brought only deception and destruction.

"Will you take me before the king?" Ivy's question cut through her thoughts.

Ruby interlaced her fingers in her lap. "If that is what you wish." She inclined her head. "Would you rather I show mercy and release you?"

What little color remained in her cheeks faded. "There is no mercy for me. It matters not what you choose. I shall never be free."

Curiosity and concern melded in her mind. "Why?"

"I am at the mercy of the Guild. They sold me to this man. My fate is in his hands unless I am caught. Then I am at the mercy of the king." Ivy's words were soft but filled with loathing.

"The Guild?" Ruby swallowed the lump of dread forming in the back of her throat. "I thought they were a legend, a myth to keep kings and emperors from misdeed."

Ivy shook her head vehemently and sighed with resignation. "The Guild is no myth."

"How long were you with them?" Ruby chose her words carefully knowing Ivy could easily lapse into silence and refuse to tell her anything. Their understanding lay stretched tenuously thin in the cold tower chamber.

"Since I was a child. I do not remember my parents or where I came from. All I know is what they taught me."

"What the Guild taught you?"

Ivy nodded. "They trained me and then sold me to the highest bidder."

"Where did you train?"

"In the mountains."

Mountains. That could be in the north along the coast leading into Scotland. "How did you come to Meradin?"

"By boat." Ivy smiled. "'Tis of no use attempting to uncover their location. I have tried and failed many times. The Guild does not wish to be uncovered, therefore it remains hidden."

Frustrated, Ruby pushed aside thoughts of the Guild and focused instead on Ivy's skills. "What did they teach you?"

"Everything I needed to be a valuable asset."

"Like seduction and espionage?" If the woman was trained by the Guild, then she would be more than a valuable asset. She was a threat. Unless Ruby could convince her to renounce her allegiance.

Ivy shrugged a shoulder and the blanket slipped free. She tugged it back into place. "Should I fail in my mission, they will send another to take my place, as well as my life. No matter where I run, I will never be safe. This is the vow of the Guild. Service until death."

A heaviness settled around Ruby's heart. During her years of solitude in the forest, she embraced the life of an outlaw, knowing it was a consequence of her decision to serve the people even should it go against the king's law. But being sold into service with no possibility of escape or redemption, the thought alone made her soul ache with despair.

"What recourse have we?" Ruby asked even though she already knew the answer in the pit of her gut.

"I finish my mission or someone else will." Ivy's brows furrowed and her eyes unfocused. When she finally met Ruby's gaze, resolve lay in their depths.

"Have you told Henry what you told me?"

A flash of regret converted to a mask of finality. Ivy schooled her features into one of serenity. "He knows not of the Guild or my past. But he is aware that regardless of whether I am brought before the king or hidden away in a prison of his choosing, I will suffer the same fate."

As much as Ivy attempted to dispel any emotional connection to Henry, she could not hide the truth from Ruby. She cared for him. More than she would ever admit. Would it be possible to use this as sufficient motivation to assure her allegiance?

"If you were given orders to kill Henry, would you follow through?" Ruby's question startled Ivy, but she recovered quickly.

"Service until death." The solemn way she spoke the words seemed disconnected, but Ivy remained steadfast.

"I see." Ruby pondered for a moment. She knew very little about the Guild and their practices. Only the stories she heard from travelers and bedtime tales Guy would weave before the fire on cold winter nights. She could not remember any of the details. *God's blood.*

"The Guild sold you to this man." Ruby mused aloud. "So then 'tis possible to buy your services?"

"I am bound to the one who purchased me until I have fulfilled my contract." Ivy reiterated. "Upon which I can be released from my bond or killed."

"Under his orders, you are to remain in my service as my maid. Correct?" Ruby continued, spinning the web with delicate threads.

"Aye." Ivy agreed.

"And as my maid, you are required to follow my command, are you not?" A smile slipped free when Ivy's eyes widened.

"Of course, ma'am."

"Then, you will remain in my service and his until we can uncover his identity and gain your freedom indefinitely." Rising to her feet, Ruby extended her hand. "Do we have an accord?"

Ivy eyed her with suspicion. "And what if he realizes my duplicity? I will be required to follow his instructions as they would supersede yours."

"Then we shall have to ensure they do not come at odds, will we not?" Ruby took the woman's hand in her own and clasped it tight. "Join me in this and we will not fail. I promise you."

"I wish I had your confidence, my queen." Ivy exhaled heavily. "What of Henry?"

"Leave him to me." While her proclamation held confidence and resolve, doubt hung over her head like a storm cloud. How could she guarantee success when so much was left out of her control? She shook it from her mind. "Come. You will return to your duties and behave as though nothing has changed. Am I clear?"

"Aye." The maid straightened with a newfound resolve.

"Come to me before you make your report, and I will have everything in place."

"What if he discovers your plan?"

Ruby pondered the possibilities repeatedly, and yet she found no other alternative without endangering more lives than necessary. "You underestimate my abilities?"

"No more than you underestimate mine…or his." Ivy studied her carefully.

"Tell no one of our agreement. Play your part." She crowded the young woman driving home the importance of her role. "Should you fail to do so, you will fall at the mercy of the king. And as you well know, death does not come easily for traitors under his rule."

Ivy's nod satisfied her well enough. Ruby pounded her fist on the door twice. The lock turned and she opened the door.

Henry's glower flickered from her to Ivy where it darkened into something more primal.

"Ivy, proceed to my chambers and prepare my gown for the feast on the morrow." Her command struck like an arrow into Henry's flesh. His face twisted, turning a deep shade of crimson in the dim lighting.

"My queen, you cannot simply release her." His hands clenched into fists as Ivy pushed past him and disappeared down the spiral staircase. "She is a traitor and must be held accountable for her actions."

"If you truly believed that, Henry, you would have taken her to Crispin without delay and demanded a swift reprimand." Ruby struck the heart of his conflict. He longed to serve with honor and loyalty, but with this unexpected emotion, he found himself torn between the two.

Henry pressed his lips together tight. His body tensed as though bracing for both an attack and a retaliation. Ruby stood her ground holding his gaze for a long moment before he swore and shook his head.

"You cannot trust her, Ruby." The words rang with his resignation.

"*We* cannot. On that point, I agree." She rested her hand on Henry's shoulder. "Watch her closely. When she leaves the castle, ensure she is followed. She is communicating with someone, and I intend to draw them out." Her grip tightened, reinforcing the importance of her instructions. "Put your best man on it. Silence and stealth are required. I do not want them knowing our part in this."

Ruby clarified the directions for how they would uncover the messenger and the man behind her mission. She explained how Ivy sent messages to the mysterious man, without including any mention of the Guild. Once she gathered more information on the mythical organization, she would relate them to Henry. But until then, he was too raw, too vulnerable when it came to Ivy. Ruby needed to maintain a barrier of separation to ensure he followed her plan exactly.

"Oh, and Henry," Ruby added, ensuring he understood the grave importance of their maintaining secrecy concerning this endeavor. "Crispin must be excluded until we uncover the perpetrator."

Henry winced at the prospect.

"Once we have a name, then we can take it before him. But he has far too much work to do to concern himself with such a small trifle."

"As you wish, my queen." Henry bent his head in submission, but not before she caught the flash of uncertainty in his expression.

"Come, let us return before we are missed." Ruby gathered her skirts and descended the narrow staircase. Upon reaching the bottom, she reaffirmed the plan in her mind and bolstered her courage.

Lying to the king would prove to be a challenge. Thankfully, she had an arsenal of tools by which to distract him. Ruby could only hope their plan succeeded for she feared the dire consequences should they fail.

Chapter Eighteen

The decision to hold council before the festival left Crispin restless. He spent most of the night preparing for the possibilities which may arise from bringing his brother before the Privy Council. He pulled every document in the archive hoping there would be something to solidify his position and legitimize his claim to the throne regardless of Francis's abdication.

He woke with his face pressed to the desk. It took him a moment to realize he was no longer alone. He softened at the sight of Ruby watching him from the doorway.

"My apologies. 'Twas not my intention to disturb you." Ruby's sultry voice brought his cock to attention.

"Your presence is a welcome distraction." He crooked his finger, beckoning her closer.

Her velvet gown brushed the floor as she walked toward him. "'Tis morning. You should prepare for your meeting with the council."

He pulled her into his lap, savoring the press of her curves against him. Her auburn curls peeked out from beneath the lace cap she wore. He brushed his fingers against her cheek. She seemed refreshed, her skin glowing.

"They will wait for me." He brushed his lips across her throat inhaling her scent.

"That will not bode well for you, my liege." She gasped when he nipped at her skin. "You must show them you take your role as king seriously."

Crispin growled. She spoke the truth, although he longed for nothing more than to spread her open on his desk and feast upon her until she writhed and begged for mercy.

Her hand cupped his cheek, forcing him to meet her gaze. He would gladly drown in their golden depths if she demanded it. This woman held him enthralled. Crispin's palm rested on her stomach. Nothing would come between them now. She belonged to him, body and soul.

"Come. I have instructed the servants to lay out your garments. You must hurry. 'Twould be unseemly for the king to arrive late for such an important meeting." Ruby pressed a kiss to his lips.

Crispin seized the opportunity and delved his tongue into her welcoming mouth. He drank from her, savoring the flicker of need igniting between them. He would never tire of this. The pleasure curled through him like a flame, making him hot and desperate.

Ruby moaned and accepted his sensual assault. She met him with the same keen desperation. When they finally broke apart, their panting breaths mingled.

He licked his lips and leaned his forehead to hers. "Go. Convey the message I shall be with them directly."

Reluctantly, Ruby rose from his lap and straightened her gown. Her hips swayed beneath the fabric making him even harder than he was already. He cursed the moment the door closed behind her. Saints above! He tugged at his hose, adjusting his now demanding cock.

Once this formality ended, he would take her against the nearest wall in celebration. God's blood, he could not sate this unnatural hunger.

He rose with an exasperated shove against the desk nearly knocking over the sturdy chair. Impatient for the charade to be finished, he proceeded to his chamber where he found his most regal garments laid neatly on the counterpane. His manservant appeared seemingly from the shadows on the other side of the bed and bowed.

With a nod, he began stripping. The servant aided him with ease, allowing Crispin's mind to wander. Even though he worried about the privy council's reaction to his brother's unexpected appearance, he felt confident they would hear Francis's story and come to the same reasonable conclusion he did.

Francis could not be king. He lacked a quintessential

requirement in Crispin's mind. Granted, his father had been quite stern in his rebuke of Crispin's prior behavior. Even threatening to remove Crispin from the line of succession completely and instead allowing his distant cousin to assume the throne. Logic could then dictate a similar possibility concerning Francis's inability to father an heir. He could simply bestow the line of succession to whomever he deemed worthy.

Crispin knew that would not include him. While Francis made no overt statement to that effect, he did not seem overly confident in Crispin's ability to rule the kingdom of Meradin. He hoped his brother's day of prayer and fasting led him to a satisfactory conclusion.

The servant secured the doublet in place, lacing the ties with careful precision. He smoothed his hands over the golden threaded royal crest embroidered on the red fabric. The eagle and the lion. His father's voice filtered through his memories.

The eagle sees things the lion cannot. But the opposite is also true. Both may be dangerous predators, and yet their strengths and perspectives differ. One can survive without the other, but united, they are unstoppable.

Over the years, Crispin slowly uncovered the deeper meaning behind the words. His father often used metaphors to teach his sons important lessons. 'Twas his attempt to unite his sons who were often locked in competition with each other for one reason or another. Even now after all that has passed, they found themselves at odds.

Crispin waved the servant away. 'Twas time to end this dilemma once and for all.

He ran his hand through his unruly hair smoothing it into some semblance of order before stepping into the corridor. Every step closer to the throne room brought his confidence to the forefront. His stride lengthened improving his posture.

The guards outside the throne room opened the door upon his approach. He found the council already seated on both sides of the aisle. With a nod of greeting, he took his place on the throne. As he studied the council, the doors opened once more.

Ruby and Vivienne entered the throne room. They both approached him, bending in subservience at his feet before taking their seats. Ruby sat to his left, and his mother to his right. Having the two most important people in his life by his side only emboldened his confidence. Infused with resolve, he nodded to the guard standing at the foot of the dais.

When the door opened, Crispin braced his hand on the arm of the gilded chair. Henry stood in the doorway, beside him the scarred monk hid beneath his hood, wearing the simple brown robes he arrived in. Together they entered the throne room.

A quiet chatter rose from the privy council seated on both sides of the room. Their curious stares followed the approach of the two men. They drew to a stop at the foot of the dais.

"Remove your hood." Crispin's command echoed through the chamber, silencing the members of the privy council.

The monk lifted the hood, letting it fall back and revealing his hideous scars.

A collective gasp rippled through the council. Crispin focused solely on the man before him.

"Tell them your name." His hand trembled, and he gripped the wood tighter, willing his body to comply.

"My name is Brother James, and I serve with the Order of Saint Bartholomew." He met Crispin's gaze boldly.

"Before that." Crispin gestured to his face.

"Prince Francis Saville, son of King Edgar and Queen Vivienne." The monk inclined his head almost imperceptibly. "Rightful heir to the throne of Meradin."

Shouts erupted throughout the council. Their words coalesced into a deep hum blocked out by the intensity of Crispin's fury. He launched to his feet and descended the stairs to meet his brother face to face.

"What proof do you have of your claim?" Crispin's question rose above the din surrounding them.

The council quieted and watched with rapt attention as the monk reached into his robes and withdrew an item. Henry drew his sword and held it to Francis's throat. Crispin glanced down at the dagger in his brother's hand.

His dagger. The dagger his brother gave him for safekeeping before he dashed into the flames. The dagger he took from the castle the night his father banished him. He studied the familiar jeweled hilt and crested blade.

"Where the devil did you get this?" Crispin growled, snatching the dagger from his hands.

"'Twas mine." His simple statement sent another wave of murmurs through the council.

Crispin caught the glimmer of amusement in his brother's eyes, but it vanished in an instant as the monk turned to the council, his hands raised in supplication.

"Honorable council, please. Silence. I shall explain all." Francis addressed both sides of the room, being sure to meet each council member's gaze in turn.

What could Crispin do but watch in horror at the sudden acquiescence of the council? He clenched the dagger tightly in his fist. If he lashed out in anger, the council would never allow him to speak.

Francis tricked him. Luring him into this moment, exposing himself as well as Crispin, forcing both their hands. One misstep would lead from check to checkmate.

He braced himself for the inevitable lies to spill from his brother's pious lips. A derisive laugh nearly escaped his throat. He swallowed it along with the bitter venom threatening to spew forth.

The council took their seats, regarding Francis with the same surprise and curiosity that gripped his mother when she realized the identity of the scarred monk. Crispin spared a glance at his mother who sat with regal bearing, her attention focused on her two sons. Her hands lay folded quietly in her lap, but he saw the tension pulling at her serene expression as she listened.

Crispin stepped back, allowing Francis to speak. He gripped the dagger in his fist and the jewels dug into his palm.

With the confidence of a true statesman, Francis uncovered the events of the night which haunted the kingdom. Every detail aligned with what he revealed to Crispin the day before. He revealed the two knights who did not survive the flames, the tunnel leading into the forest, and the unfortunate repercussions of his injuries.

Crispin suppressed a grin of triumph when a collective murmur rose from the council at the revelation of Francis's inability to produce an heir. Such a deficit would surely guide them in his favor when he revealed Ruby's increasing state.

"I have prayed at length and fasted to aid in deciding what steps I must take to move forward in my service to God and my kingdom." Francis bowed his head in a show of humility.

The Master of Coin rose to his feet. "Why did you not come forward sooner? At least to acknowledge you survived the fire."

"The brotherhood accepted me without hesitation. My injuries were extensive. It took a year for me to recoup the use of my voice. The recovery of my memory took me much longer." Francis faced each council member in turn as he spoke. "'Twas only over the past year the fog has lifted from my mind, allowing me to piece together the details of my past and that harrowing night."

Squaring his shoulders, Crispin bit his tongue to keep from calling out the obvious lies. How could one have no recollection of their past and then miraculously recover such vivid details with disturbing certainty? His lip twitched, but he remained silent, storing every lie within his arsenal.

The council member resumed his seat seemingly satisfied with Francis's response.

This time the gray-bearded advisor Crispin's father often leaned upon for guidance rose from his seat near the dais. His gaze roamed over Francis before settling on Crispin. A measured appraisal.

Crispin stood unflinching and proud.

"Do you intend to abdicate your claim to the throne?" The wise councilman cut directly to the bone without flowery words meant to ease the blunt pain of such a question.

"God has chosen a challenging path for me to travel through this life," Francis responded without hesitation. "I believe He has a higher purpose for me."

Crispin's conscience eased at the statement, but his body tensed as though sensing a battle on the horizon.

"I do not claim to understand the providence of the Divine,

but He has led me to this moment through these specific trials for a reason." Francis turned his gaze to Crispin. "I cannot in good conscience abdicate my claim to the throne."

Overlapping conversations burst free at Francis's statement, filling the throne room with raised voices crying shock and outrage. Crispin scanned the faces of the council before glancing at his mother whose face paled and then Ruby, who sat with her hand over her mouth and eyes wide.

A rush of possessive rage pulsed through him. He spun around to face his brother.

"Silence!" His command rang through the room like a crack of thunder.

The conversations quickly lapsed into murmurs and then faded completely. Crispin took a steady measure of every face in the room before finally resting on Francis.

"You intend to take the throne?" Crispin's question issued a challenge one could hardly refute.

"I shall go where the Lord leads me." Francis's cryptic reply drew across his skin like talons cutting flesh.

"What is the desire of your heart, brother?" Crispin stepped close, searching for the deception he knew lurked in the depths of the monk's sainted soul.

"'Tis my desire to serve," Francis replied simply.

Crispin ground his teeth so hard his jaw ached. "As the King of Meradin, I will grant your heart's desire to serve God for the rest of your days, but in exchange, you must abdicate any right to the throne."

"Until God moves me to do so, I am His humble servant." The monk bowed his head. "I cannot deny my birthright until the Lord instructs me to do so."

The weight of his words settled around Crispin like a loadstone tied to his neck. He stepped back, stunned and infuriated by the events unfolding before him. He should have killed him while he slept in his cell and disposed of the body.

"If I may, your majesty." A lone voice pierced his soul. The sweet cadence soothed his rising anguish. *Ruby.* He turned as she rose from her seat and clasped her hands together. She stood tall and proud, her chin lifted high, her tender gaze resting on the men before her. Never had she looked so regal. His heart ached with pride and longing.

Pushing aside his thoughts, Crispin motioned for her to continue with a wave of his hand.

"Perhaps a compromise can be met." Ruby descended the dais to stand beside Francis and Crispin. "Crispin remains on the throne, and Francis is permitted to live out his days in service to God with the brotherhood."

"Our law states he must abdicate the throne for the next in line of succession to take his place." The Master of Coin clarified with a dismissive scoff.

"Who makes the laws?" Ruby asked pointedly. "The king, upon the direction and consultation of his council." She faced each of them in turn. "Surely this is an extenuating circumstance in which a compromise can be met. The brotherhood serves the kingdom as well as God. Brother James—Francis—has been an important and valuable addition to their ministry. Surely his time spent in their service is worth consideration."

"And what if he wakes one day and decides to take the throne, as is his right?" another council member added.

Over my dead, rotting corpse, Crispin thought with conviction. No one would steal this from him. No one.

Ruby's gentle touch brought his thoughts out of the darkness. He glanced at her hand resting on his fist with the dagger clenched tightly inside it. He relaxed his grip, allowing her to take the dagger.

"The council should take some time to deliberate these matters." Ruby's calm statement eased his concern. She was giving them time to deliberate and not react out of impulse. "Tonight is the feast of the harvest. Let us celebrate the bounty and prosperity while taking the time to ponder these pressing matters with rational discourse."

Murmured agreements emanated from the council.

"In a sennight, the council can convene once more with a solution." Ruby smiled, casting a spell over those in the room, Crispin included. "Until then, Francis is welcome to remain as our guest and join in the celebration."

"Hear, hear!" The gray-haired councilman shouted. "I am in agreement with the queen. Her wise proposition will allow us to make the best decision for the kingdom."

The rest of the council added their agreement, some more readily than others.

"Not a word of this discussion leaves this room until we reach a satisfactory agreement. Is that understood?" Crispin waited until every person in the room nodded in agreement and ended the debate with a simple dismissal. "This council is adjourned until seven days hence. Now to prepare for the celebration."

Francis held Crispin's gaze with determination. A myriad of conflicting emotions swam in the depths of his brother's eyes. Tension burned hot between them.

Ruby stepped in front of Crispin, breaking the contact with an audible snap. "You are welcome to remain in the castle and join in the festivities."

"I thank you for your kindness, ma'am." Francis bowed. "But I must return to my brothers and tend to those in need. I shall return when I am summoned."

"As you wish." Ruby stood like a barrier between them until Francis vacated the room, escorted by Henry.

The rest of the council followed behind them, leaving Crispin alone in the throne room with his mother and his wife. When the door sealed, Crispin wished he had something in his hand to throw or someone to strike.

Unease and uncertainty churned in his gut souring his mood. He paced the length of the room and ran his hand through his hair.

"What ails you, my king?" Ruby stood in his path. "I thought that went quite well."

"The words spoken in this room will not remain contained for long." Crispin faced his mother and Ruby. "'Tis only a matter of time before they reveal Francis is alive. If they have not done so already." He flexed his hands, wishing for the comforting weight of his weapon.

"You instructed them to remain silent." Vivienne stepped closer. "They will respect your wishes, for the moment."

"The whispers will begin before the day is through. Simple gossip spreads like a plague through the castle." Crispin furrowed his brow in thought. There was naught he could do to stop it short of threats. "When we arrive at the feast, every guest will know Francis is alive and refusing to relinquish claim to the throne."

"What if we gave them something else to ponder?" Ruby's countenance brightened. "This evening at the feast, we shall announce our wonderful news. The promise of an heir is sure to draw the attention and celebration of the people."

Crispin scoffed. "You underestimate how beloved my brother once was among the people."

"Then I shall instruct my maids to plant the revelation in the ears of every servant they encounter. By nightfall, the whole of the kingdom will speak only of the king and his heir." He admired the confidence in her plan. Ruby continued, "No one but the council has seen Francis. He will not be in attendance of festival nor the feast."

"The plan may work if we can direct the attention elsewhere." A ray of light engulfed his soul. He pulled Ruby into his arms and kissed her soundly. When he pulled away, her unfocused gaze locked with his, making his heart swell with pride and his cock with need.

Vivienne cleared her throat reminding him of her presence. "Perhaps you should speak with your maids and set your plan into motion."

Ruby kissed him once more before leaving the throne room. Once the door closed behind her, Crispin felt the weight of the surmounting conflict pulling him into the darkness again.

"I have seen that look before, my son." Vivienne rested her hand on his shoulder. "Do not allow those dark thoughts to tempt you."

A charming smile broke upon his lips. "I have done my part. Upheld my end of the agreement. No harm will come to Francis." He dropped all pretense when he met her unyielding gaze.

"You have done well thus far." She cupped his chin in her delicate hand, the grip stronger than it should have been. "But you have a propensity to underestimate the challenges before you. At some point, you will need to make a decision. I pray you choose wisely."

"Have you no faith in me, Mother?" Her words encircled him like an ancient riddle written in foreign text, but he ignored them, focusing on the small glimmer of hope shining just out of reach.

"There will be countless challenges you face in your life, Crispin. I fear they will only grow in intensity over the coming months." She released her grip. "Stand firm and follow your heart. Do not give in to the darkness lurking in your soul."

Without elaborating on what her cryptic words might infer, Vivienne strode from the room leaving Crispin to ponder their implications.

He climbed the dais and sat on the gilded chair where his father once sat. Francis would never steal this from him. It would take an act of God to remove Crispin from his rightful place.

Once Francis returned to the monastery, Crispin would place it under constant surveillance. All visitors tracked and questioned. If Francis wished to play politics, who was he to dissuade him. He relished the opportunity to wield his power over his sainted brother.

If they could not come to a satisfactory compromise within a week, then drastic measures must be taken to ensure the monarchy endured. Should Francis's identity be revealed to the kingdom, loyalties would be tested. Brother would turn against brother. The kingdom would split with indecision. A civil war would rip the nation apart.

Crispin would never allow that to happen. He would sully his hands and his reputation before he allowed Meradin to be torn between two kings. There would only ever be one king. Him.

Even if that meant he needed to remove his brother permanently.

Chapter Nineteen

The shadows offered the most comfort. When the doors opened admitting the guests for the feast, Henry lingered in the darkness behind the large pillar. The vantage point offered a full view of the great hall. Perfect for allowing him to watch without being noticed.

His dark blue doublet and black tunic allowed him to move freely through the shadows without drawing attention to himself. Henry spent much of the day finalizing rotations for the guards in preparation for the festival. After the disastrous meeting with the privy council earlier in the day, he personally escorted Francis from the premises per the king's instructions.

The guests filtered into the great hall, filling the vaulted ceiling with boisterous conversation and lively music. He studied each guest in turn, gauging their station by the cut of their clothes and their risk by the weapons they carried. Guards held positions at each entrance to the castle while archers walked the walls. Henry ensured every possible weakness was removed or strengthened. This was his responsibility, and he would be damned if he failed his king.

A pair of maids walked past him. They jumped when he shifted, materializing out of the shadows. Their nervous laughter followed behind them as they hurried toward the guests.

Henry folded his arms across his chest and leaned against the pillar. No matter how hard he tried to push her from his mind. His thoughts drifted to Ivy without effort, driving him to distraction and frustration. He longed for her, but he could not shake the indisputable fact he could not trust her.

The seed of doubt in his mind took root and from it sprouted a vine of suspicion. It curled around his heart constricting it with every breath. Although he had no confession and no proof of her intentions, it was difficult to shake the blossoming dread deep in his gut. Something lay upon the horizon, although he could not see or name it, he could not dismiss it.

Although Henry had not seen many battles firsthand, he encountered many minor conflicts during his service to the kingdom of Meradin. The twisting of uncertainty in his gut led him quite effectively through these difficulties. Much like the night of the fire when his intuition led him away from the inn. He could not fathom the reason why until much later. Almost as though a hand reached down from the heavens and touched his soul, guiding him down a different path ensuring his protection.

He shook his head. Such a feeling seemed almost contradictory to his obligation, and yet how many times had it saved them in the past. This time, the feeling pulled him deeper into the unknown instead of away from it. Henry feared Ruby's decision to release Ivy set them on an irreversible course. They were sailing into the heart of a tempest. Henry could do naught but hold fast and brace for the oncoming storm.

The music faded abruptly, pulling Henry from his thoughts. A flash of gold and red over the heads of the crowd told him the king and queen arrived amidst their guests. He shifted his position to ensure a direct view of the elevated area where the king's table sat at the head of the room.

Ruby shone like the sun rising over the mountains. Her vibrant hair lay hidden beneath a gilded snood studded with pearls. The contrasting blue and red of her gown hid her curves but complimented her shape while emphasizing her position in an understated manner. The colors lay divided by a gold ribbon stitched along the seam. A golden brooch of the Saville royal crest, a lion and an eagle, held her mantle in place over her left shoulder.

Crispin wore a matching doublet and mantle. The same crest stitched across his chest. They complimented each other perfectly down to their crowns.

Henry never saw such an exquisite display. Even Crispin's coronation and their wedding had not been as elaborate or calculated as this. He watched with unease as Crispin took

Ruby's hand and placed a kiss on her knuckles.

The tender gesture produced a sigh from various quarters of the crowd. What most would view as a loving moment between the king and queen, held a multitude of layers and meaning. The kingdom knew nothing of the turmoil churning within the castle walls. All for the better.

"Loyal subjects and gracious guests." Crispin's greeting shook the rafters. His charming smile blinded Henry from where he stood across the room. "I bid you welcome. The harvest festival is a time of celebration for the bounty granted by the Lord."

Henry narrowed his gaze and focused on the king's words knowing full well Crispin would utilize his unrelenting charm to distract and entertain. Years of friendship and undying fealty created a firm disillusionment protecting him from the effects of its use.

"As we come together to revel in the bounty of the harvest, let us also bask in the joyous miracle of life." Crispin nodded with a wide grin. "Come the spring, amid the miracle of the blossoming wildflowers and ripening fields, we shall have even more cause to celebrate. A new heir to the throne of Meradin."

Raucous cheers shook the walls. Henry braced himself, refraining from clamping his hands over his ears to block the deafening noise surrounding him. As the people cheered, Crispin preened. Ruby stood beside him, her gaze fixed firmly on her husband, cheeks flushed with what one could only expect to be happiness and pride.

"Let us eat, drink, and be merry!" Crispin lifted his chalice in a toast.

"Hear, hear!" The calls filled the room. "Long live the king! Long live the queen!"

Henry relaxed against the pillar when Crispin and Ruby took their seats. The crowd followed their lead and fell into amicable conversation with their neighbors.

As the feast progressed, Henry wandered the length of the room, remaining along the wall tucked out of sight. Every passing maid drew his attention. Yet none of them held it.

Since Ruby released Ivy, he followed her every movement, until astonishingly, she vanished completely. He bit back the resentment burning inside him. 'Twas possible she fled the castle the moment she saw her opportunity. She was a liability, an unverified unknown. He should have taken her before Crispin and saved them all. As much as he respected and admired Ruby, she often let her heart overrule her head. Her decision to release Ivy may have been one borne of mercy rather than thoughtful contemplation.

The unease returned with a vengeance. Henry rested his hand on the pommel of his sword. It gave him some measure of comfort but did nothing to dispel the onslaught of tension filling him.

He slipped out the door, taking the opportunity to make his rounds. The main gate and rear guardhouse lay in blissful silence. He walked the balustrade, ensuring the men kept their vigilant watch.

The crisp air revitalized him. He breathed deep, savoring the oncoming bite of winter. He climbed down the ladder to the bailey, stretching his arms overhead. Servants and guests came and went from the great hall.

Henry walked along the wall, stopping to pet the hound lying outside the stables. While the kingdom celebrated, he found himself incapable of joining in the festivities. His gaze roamed the courtyard once more. All lay at peace.

Still, he could not shake the unrelenting chill surrounding him unrelated to the weather.

As he neared the main gate, a flurry of activity drew his attention.

"I must speak with him," the man persisted with the guard.

"What seems to be the trouble here?" Henry asked, stepping out from the shadows.

"He is demanding to speak with the king." The guard lowered his sword allowing the man into the bailey.

"I am the king's High Steward. State your business." Henry crossed his arms and studied the slender man wearing peasant's clothes.

"A group of men came through our village." The man dropped his gaze. "They bore the signet of Balmont."

Henry straightened at the mention of his family's name. "What village?"

"Fenrick, a two-day journey along the king's road."

"Does that not lie on the border with Wales?" Henry pictured the map in his mind. His family had been quite adept at avoiding attention for the past two months, why would they suddenly show themselves.

"Aye, your grace." The man bowed. "They pilfered stores from our grain and half the livestock in the village." He twisted his hat between his hands. "There is not enough to get us through winter. The village fears they will return for the rest."

Henry nodded while his mind processed the new information. It would take several days for him to gather enough men and travel to Fenrick. Perhaps he could send a small contingent with supplies to hold the village until he completed his duties here and was able to join them.

"Come in, eat, rest from your journey. I shall present your case to the king personally." Henry nodded to the guards who resumed their post and led the man toward the great hall. Inside, the revelry continued. Music and laughter mingled with the scent of roast mutton, braised pork, and copious amounts of wine and ale.

He directed the man to sit at the far table and pulled aside a servant with instructions to serve him directly. Then he wove around the tables, his intent focused on the king's table.

"My liege." Henry knelt beside Crispin's chair and bowed his head.

"There you are. Hiding in the shadows, were you?" Crispin hid his grin behind his chalice.

Henry studied his friend's face for a long moment, briefly imagining driving his fist hard into his nose. He shook the thought away and cleared his throat. "There is a messenger arrived from Fenrick, a town on the king's road near Wales. It seems my family has come out from whatever hole they were hiding in. They stole the winter stores from the village."

Crispin's amused grin faded and his gaze hardened into ice. "When was this?"

"Several days ago, sire. 'Tis a two-day journey to Fenrick." Henry kept his voice low. "With your permission, sire, I would like to send a small garrison with some supplies to Fenrick. I will join them once my duties here are fulfilled."

"You will remain by my side until we conclude our dealings with the monk." Crispin hissed beneath his breath. "Send supplies and some soldiers as you will, but you shall not leave this castle until I permit you. Is that understood?"

"As you command, my liege." Henry held Crispin's gaze. They lay locked in a tense battle of silence until a soft voice interjected.

"If you will pardon me, I must retire." Ruby appeared beside him.

Crispin and Henry rose simultaneously.

"Would you like me to join you?" Crispin asked, offering his hand.

She blushed and shook her head. "Please stay and enjoy your celebration. I am simply overwhelmed by the heat."

"May I escort you, my queen?" Henry offered, ignoring Crispin's glare.

"'Tis quite unnecessary. I am capable of finding the way to my chamber." She dipped into a curtsey and turned to leave the great hall.

"I shall speak to the man from Fenrick and arrange the details." Crispin remained focused on the doorway where Ruby stood moments before. "Follow her. If she attempts to leave the castle, you have your instructions."

The foreboding filled him once more, but Henry gave a curt nod of understanding. He pulled aside a servant with instructions to have their guest meet with the king after the meal.

As he climbed the stairs toward the queen's chamber, he ignored the increased sense of unease prickling the hairs on the back of his neck. He heard Ruby's voice through the door and leaned against the wall beside it. If she chose to leave the castle, she would have to go through him first. Though this time he could not fault her for wanting to escape, if only for a moment.

Chapter Twenty

The night passed with an agonizing tediousness, leaving Ruby restless. While the feast itself was a rousing success, she could not stomach the scent of the roasted meat. Her stomach churned at the thought of it.

Henry's arrival gave her the perfect opportunity to excuse herself from the festivities. With Crispin distracted by other matters, she was able to take her leave without him worrying over her condition. She needed to be away from the overwhelming aromas filling the great hall and take some time to clear her mind.

She paced her chamber well into the night waiting for Crispin's arrival. When he never appeared, she attempted to sleep. The stillness crawled beneath her skin, leaving her unable to find peace in slumber. She wished she had a potion to help soothe her stomach and aid in her sleep.

Frustrated, Ruby rose from the tangled bedding and donned a simple kirtle followed by her leather boots. She braided her hair over her shoulder and fastened the belt around her waist securing the dagger to her side. After retrieving the wool cloak from the wardrobe, she pulled it over her shoulders.

A ride through the forest would surely cure her of all ailments. Before she became queen, it served her well enough. Perhaps she could avoid having to take an escort. They drew more attention than they offered protection.

Quietly, she opened the door and stepped into the corridor. Her feet tangled beneath her stumbling over something lying across her threshold. Bracing herself against the fall, she collided with something warm and more forgiving than the stone floor.

"Where in the devil are you off to at this ungodly hour?" Henry held her firmly against him.

She drew back, stunned at his presence and their situation. "I should ask why you are guarding my door, but I believe I already know the reason." She righted her skirts and rose to her feet. "Have you been out here all night?"

Henry stared up at her for a moment. "I believe you already know the answer to that question as well."

Irritation filled her. Would Crispin never allow her to do as she pleased without having her every step dogged by one of his loyal hounds? She watched Henry rise and stretch his arms overhead, stifling a yawn behind his hand. The poor man seemed as restless and weary as she with recent events. Her heart softened at the shared similarity.

"Am I confined to the castle then?" She offered a sly smile hoping to appeal to his own need for a reprieve.

He rubbed his hand along his scruff-covered jaw. "That depends upon your escort and his willingness to disobey a direct order." His eyes twinkled with amusement. "The king will be quite displeased to know his queen is not safe behind these walls."

"'Tis a pity. I find riding before dawn quite invigorating and restorative." She held his gaze. "If only there were a strong, capable guard who might allow me this small concession."

Henry shook his head and chuckled. "Saints preserve me. We must return before the sun, and the king catches us beyond these walls."

Ruby bounded down the hall, her heart lighter than it had been all week. These infrequent moments of escape allowed her to retain what remained of her sanity. No matter what Vivienne said, she would never be fully comfortable in her role as queen. Not when the forest and the echoing call of her past freedoms called to her from beyond the horizon.

She followed Henry down the hall and out into the courtyard. The castle lay enshrouded by the pre-dawn darkness. Not a soul stirred within the bailey. A waning moon shone down from the sky casting its muted light across the stables.

"Remain here," Henry instructed, leaving her to saddle her horse.

Ginger gave a gentle whicker at the sight of her mistress. Ruby stroked the horse's nose and pressed her face against the mare's neck. "I have not forgotten you."

Quietly, she groomed her mount before lifting the saddle into place. The sound of approaching footsteps made her pause and crouch behind the stall door.

"'Tis I." Henry's low voice filled her with relief. When she peered over the stall door, she saw Henry was not alone. "This is Connor. He shall accompany us as a precaution."

Ruby nodded to the knight. How much did he know?

"Your majesty." Connor bowed.

She pressed her lips together and scowled at Henry who inclined his head. They worked in silence as the men retrieved their horses.

With skilled ease, the two men saddled their mounts, and altogether they led them into the yard. Once they were seated, Henry reined his horse around and pressed his fingers to his lips. He then led the way toward the postern gate. Connor followed behind.

The guards blocked their path, but after a few whispered instructions, they allowed them to slip through the gate and out into the forest.

Ruby came alongside Henry as they wove along the trail leading toward the king's road. "What did you tell them?"

"We are escorting a maid on an errand for the queen." She barely caught a glimpse of Henry's smile through the thick shadows. "Do not concern yourself. We shall return before we are missed."

The path widened as they approached the main road. Henry nudged his horse into a trot. Ruby grinned and followed his lead. Eager as her mistress, Ginger launched into a canter to keep pace with Henry's gelding.

The cool morning air brushed over her face revitalizing and comforting as it bit into her skin. She nudged Ginger faster. Connor maintained his proximity, his horse's hoofbeats echoing behind her, mirroring the thundering of her heart.

They rounded a small bend and spilled out onto the king's road. Ruby kicked Ginger's flanks urging her into a gallop. Without effort, her mare overtook Henry's gelding. His curse faded into the distance.

Her hood slid back and her hair pulled free from the braid as they sped through the forest. Freedom. It beckoned her with sweet unfulfilled promises and filled her heart with fresh dreams of a brighter future. She raced down the road untroubled by the turmoil plaguing the kingdom and her fate.

She longed for the days of her youth spent riding breakneck through the forest, gathering herbs with Marian, and practicing her swordsmanship with Guy. Tears pricked her eyes, but the wind caught them up in an instant. These moments, small snatches of freedom, would be her salvation. She required it for her very survival, like one needed air or water. It fed her soul as well as her spirit. No one could steal this from her. Not the king, not the court, not even the devil himself.

The road curved ahead. Highlighted by a glint of moonlight through the trees, a dark object shifted just beyond the bend. Ruby eased Ginger down to a trot, allowing Henry and Connor to catch her up.

"God's blood, teeth, and bones, Ruby!" Henry swore beneath his breath as he came alongside her. "How am I to protect you if you race off like an unruly child hellbent on mischief?"

"You act as though I cannot care for myself." She chuckled at his exasperated sigh. "I am as well adept as swordplay as you are, or do you forget what they called me before I became queen?"

"Lady of the Forest is a moniker bestowed upon a legend." Henry ran his hand through his hair. "I have not had the pleasure of experiencing your skills firsthand, however seeing as you have no sword and no bow, this puts you at a distinct disadvantage should we encounter trouble."

The horses slowed to a walk as they approached the curve. Henry held up his hand, bringing them to a stop. Ginger danced in circles as Henry inspected the large object before them. A wagon stood broadside effectively blocking the narrow curve.

"Stay back. Connor." Henry gestured to Ruby before he drew his sword and approached the wagon. His horse shifted uncomfortably as if sensing the tension of its rider. "Who goes there?"

The hair on Ruby's neck rose as a cold breeze shifted through the trees and brushed its icy fingertips along her skin. She gripped her dagger's hilt, prepared to fight but braced to flee should she need to do so. Her body tensed as she scanned the tree line.

Connor drew closer with his sword drawn. "Stay close, my queen."

The wind ruffled the drying leaves, breaking them loose from their branches. Ruby's heart pounded, echoing in her ears making it difficult to tell if she heard footsteps or merely figments of her imagination.

Ginger snorted and pawed at the ground impatiently. She shifted her feet and spun around only adding to the building tension surrounding them. Ruby held the reins tight and grasped the saddle firmly between her thighs.

An owl's call drifted through trees. The haunting sound sent a shiver down her spine.

"Go! Make haste!" Henry shouted.

Ruby dug her heels into Ginger's sides, driving the horse into a gallop. As they raced in the direction of the castle, she glanced over her shoulder in time to see dark figures emerge from the forest and hear the clang of swords striking together.

She wanted to help them but the seed of warning had been planted. There would be no point if she were to sacrifice herself when they gave her the opportunity to escape. Urging Ginger faster, she crouched over the horse's neck.

A shadow of darkness covered the road ahead. Too late, Ruby saw the line of horsemen obscuring her only escape. Ginger reared on her hind legs, knocking Ruby from her seat. She landed with a thud on her backside and scrambled to her feet. The riders surrounded her as Ginger bolted beyond the blockade, heading toward the safety of the castle.

The brush lay thick on either side of the road, preventing her from evading the oncoming assault. She drew her dagger from her hip and gripped it tight in her palm, keeping it hidden in the folds of her cloak until they came close enough for her to strike with deadly accuracy.

"Come on then. Cowards. Face me," she growled, trying to see their faces in the darkness. Four riders blocked her with their massive destriers. These were not built for speed, but they were as strong as they were obedient. The hulking stallions crept closer.

Ruby stumbled back a few steps nearly tripping over her cloak. Fear gripped her throat, choking her and smothering the curses as they formed on her lips.

A rush of thundering hooves from behind her and she was lifted airborne by a pair of strong arms. Draped across the saddle, she clung to her rescuer.

"Hold on tight." Henry secured her arms around him, careful of the dagger when it nicked his sleeve. He turned his attention to the mysterious riders. "Hiyahhhh!" He drove his heels into his gelding's sides, and they shot toward the massive beasts with the speed of an arrow loosed from a longbow.

The destriers danced across the path with no intent to move. Ruby buried her face in Henry's chest and clung to him with all her might. The sound of hooves and the squeal of angered stallions pierced the night. She hazarded a peek at the carnage and caught a glimpse of Connor clashing with two of the assailants astride their steeds.

An opening appeared in the road providing the perfect escape. His horse spun and collided with one of the stallions knocking Henry back. Ruby's grip broke free, and she slid from the saddle. A scream wrenched from her throat. A firm arm wrapped around her waist before she hit the ground.

"I have her," the man holding her growled to his companions. In the shadows, she could make out none of her captor's features.

"Over my corpse." Ruby drove her dagger into the man's torso. He screamed in pain, and she tumbled from his grip.

When she hit the ground, she gathered her skirts and ran as fast as she could into the tree line. Branches tore at her hair and clothing. One slashed at her face leaving a stinging warmth. She pressed onward hoping to lose them in the thicket.

Shouts and echoes of battle continued behind her. She pushed further into the forest and away from the noise. If she could find the nearest village or even a farm, she could take refuge.

Every breath burned in her chest. Her side ached, her legs trembled, and still, she persisted. They could not find her. She harbored no delusions as to why they would want her. She was the queen, and the king had more enemies than friends at the moment.

Henry tried to warn her. Guilt stabbed her. *Henry.* He fought valiantly to protect her. She would never forgive herself if she caused his death with her careless dismissal and selfish demands. The brush thinned, making it easier to walk. She leaned against a tree and took a deep breath, trying to ease the pull in her side.

She glanced over her shoulder. The forest lay quiet around her. Gone were the sounds of swords clashing and men shouting. Even the sound of the horses had faded. Ruby pressed a hand to her racing heart and took several calming breaths. Somehow she needed to find her way back to the castle. It could not be far, but she would need to remain hidden in the trees and stay off the roads.

Once she was able to think clearly, Ruby began her slow journey back to the castle. The sky turned a dusky blue overhead signaling sunrise was just over the horizon. She used it to guide her way back to the castle being careful of any roads or trails she may encounter.

When the castle came into view through the trees, relief filled her. She wiped the dried blood from her cheek with her sleeve and quickened her pace. The sun warmed her as it streamed through the bare branches overhead.

With a murmur of thanks to the heavens, Ruby slowly climbed the incline leading to the postern gate. She slipped and caught her skirt on a branch which tore her skirt and left a gash on her thigh. Pain ripped through her, and she collapsed against a nearby oak tree.

A twig snapped in the distance. Ruby straightened and reached for her dagger, swearing when she found the sheath empty. She crept forward and reached for a fallen oak branch to use as a weapon.

A flash of blinding pain shot through the back of her head and radiated down her limbs. She tumbled to the ground grasping to keep ahold of consciousness when her body fell upon the decaying leaves littering the forest floor. The scent of the earth and blood filled her nostrils.

Ruby groaned, struggling to open her eyes and call for help. But no words came. Her body collapsed uselessly to the ground. Her lids sank heavily, obscuring her vision.

Chapter Twenty-One

Crispin could not remember the last time he slept so deeply. The morning sun shone through the windows of his chamber, casting glittering rays of light across the opulent surroundings. He barely remembered returning to his chambers the evening before.

His feet first led him to Ruby's door, where he found Henry braced across the doorway fast asleep. It would have been within his right to wake him and send him away. Yet the reminder of his bride's pale complexion at supper halted his hand. She deserved some rest after the past few days. They would have plenty of time to spend in each other's company over the coming years.

Instead, he dragged himself to his chamber and threw himself onto the bed fully clothed and careless. He regretted it upon waking. The doublet constricted his chest.

Sitting up, he unfastened the tedious buttons on the doublet finally able to breathe with ease when it opened. He peeled it from his shoulders and tossed it aside. Once he stripped the rest of his clothes, he crossed to the washbasin and splashed the cold water onto his face.

The sting of the liquid faded as it warmed and dripped onto his chest. He repeated the action until his faculties revived. A hot bath would have been preferable, but he had little time for it.

The festival began at midday. He and Ruby would join the rest of the court at the opening of the celebration in the village square. For the first time in his life, he anticipated the harvest festival with pleasure rather than scorn. In years past, he desired more to spend the event sequestered in a tavern far away with a pint and a willing wench than attend the annual event.

This was different. He was king. Ruby was his queen. Together they would attend the festival and join in the revelry.

Perhaps they could steal off to some quiet corner and he could claim her during the celebration. The thought alone heated his blood.

He dried himself with a cloth and selected fresh garments from the wardrobe. Within moments he dressed and pulled on a simple doublet with a gold eagle embroidered on the shoulder. A gift from his mother two years past. His fingertips grazed the gilded threads. She stitched it with her own hands. It was only fitting to wear it in her honor on this day.

After pulling on his boots, Crispin ran his hand through his unruly hair and paused to inspect his reflection in the mirror hanging on the far wall. The black fabric amplified the dark locks lying in waves across his pale skin. Regal. Powerful. *Me.*

His crooked smile reflected before he took his leave. Down the corridor, he paused outside Ruby's chamber. The doorway stood vacant. Henry had abandoned his post.

Crispin knocked, ignoring the knot forming in the pit of his stomach. No reply came from within. He opened the door and searched the room quickly only to find it empty and the fire burned down to smoldering embers. Perhaps she had risen early in the excitement of the festivities.

Expectant and growing more agitated by the moment, Crispin searched the castle, starting with the most obvious possibilities to locate his queen. When he reached the stables and found her horse missing from its stall, he leaned on the door and hung his head in thought. Where in the devil could she be? Henry's horse was gone as well.

"What the devil..." He muttered beneath his breath. Seeking out the stable master, he pinned the man to the nearest post demanding answers. "Who took those horses out?"

"They were gone when we woke, my liege," the man murmured mid-bow. "I have sent some men to search for them, but none have returned."

Crispin abandoned the stables, fear twisting in his gut. How many times had he told her to remain in the castle? Even though he gave Henry instructions to allow her a small concession should she need to escape her confines for a short while, they should have returned within an hour, two at the most.

If the stablemaster spoke the truth, they left well before dawn.

He checked the main gate with no success. The postern gate reported Henry left with a maid and another knight in the early morning before the sun rose. Several other servants used the postern gate that morning, but no one returned for none were granted entrance.

Suppressing his rage, Crispin stalked around the castle. There could be a hundred reasons they had not returned. Perhaps she insisted they visit her mother or stopped to gather herbs. He refused to contemplate the other possibilities. She knew better than to approach the monastery with the current tensions brewing.

As he entered the open bailey, a commotion at the gate pulled him from his thoughts. The guards parted and two soldiers carried a man between them. Blood dripped from the gash on his head. His eyes widened, the right swollen and purple, at the sight of Crispin. He broke free from the guards holding him and fell to his knees before his king.

"Your majesty." The split on his protruding lip made his speech nearly incomprehensible. "I have failed you."

"What happened?" Crispin studied the young knight. He recognized him from the training grounds, but his name escaped his memory.

"We were ambushed. The duke has been taken. I would have been killed had it not been for a passing patrol." The man swayed but maintained his position. "The queen escaped on foot into the forest. The patrol is searching for her as we speak."

Hope and dismay filled Crispin in equal measures. He refrained from grasping the man and shaking him until every detail fell free.

"Someone, fetch the healer." He pointed to the two guards who escorted the wounded man into the bailey. "Carry him into the castle. Have him tended."

He spun around to face the crowd forming around him. "If any of you has a whisper of information, now is the moment to bring it forward." He clenched his hands into fists and raised his voice. "Bring me every soldier, every knight in the kingdom. Scour the forest. Set blockades on the roads."

The crowd around him grew as did Crispin's unbridled rage. "Not a soul will rest until the queen is recovered. Go!"

The masses around him scattered in every direction. Crispin's chest ached at the thought of his Ruby lying wounded or dead in the forest. He would interrogate the knight once the healer gave him a restorative tonic.

The captain of the guard stood by his side. "I have sent every available man out as you have commanded, sire."

"Send Matthew, the blacksmith's apprentice, with a message for Marian, the queen's mother to come to the castle, post-haste." The captain bowed and retreated without delay.

"What has happened?" His mother appeared in the bailey, her wide eyes scouring the chaos in the yard.

"Ambush." Crispin scowled at the guilt entwining around his pride. Had he joined her in her chambers, this would never have happened. He would have kept her safe. In his arms. In his bed. Damn it. He pushed it aside. "Ruby has vanished. Henry has been taken. They were out riding. One of the escorts has returned, but he is gravely injured."

"Saints preserve us." Vivienne crossed herself. "I shall tend to the wounded man. Perhaps has information that may serve us well in our search."

Crispin took his mother's hand in his own and gripped it tight in acknowledgment. Words failed him. Her strength infused him with confidence. They would find her.

A shout from the postern gate sent him into a run. The small cluster of guards parted as he approached.

"What have you found?" Crispin demanded at the sight of their pensive stares.

One of the guards held up a strip of dark green cloth. "I found it just over the hill, my liege. There was sign of a struggle. This was caught on a jagged branch."

He snatched the fabric from the man's hand. Ruby's, he would stake his life on it. "Did you find anything else?"

"Aye, your majesty." The man offered a leather sheath with a glittering ruby adorning it attached to a belt.

There was no denying these items belonged to Ruby. She had been taken on his doorstep.

"Scour the countryside. Find her." He hissed the command and the men scattered.

Crispin squeezed the belt and fabric in his fist. He returned to the yard to find the three horses had returned. Fire burned hot and bright inside him. He would hunt down these fiends and punish them repeatedly, sparing them the reprieve of death. They would pay for their brazen abduction of his queen.

Inside the great hall, the servants rushed to and fro. Guests filtered into the room, whispers and murmurs filling the space. As more entered the room, his agitation and fury intensified.

"*Out!*" His patience erupted, spilling forth and silencing all in his presence. "There will be no celebration this day. No conversation. No joy. No laughter. No revelry. There will be no peace until my queen is recovered." He slammed his fist on the table. "If you intend to do nothing but sit on your pampered arses, then get out of my sight!"

A flurry of movement commenced at his enraged proclamation. He cared not for their placating words or their simpering complaints. They could all go to the devil and burn.

Until Ruby was returned unharmed, the kingdom would not rest. No one would rest. He would overturn every rock, scour every hillside, and question every man, woman, and child in Meradin to find his queen.

Someone in this castle knew of her propensities. They knew her habits. They watched and waited for the opportunity to strike. He would question the wounded knight, and then he would join the search, starting with the location where they were ambushed.

Crispin would not sleep until he found her. His hunger for blood and vengeance increased the longer he dwelled on the matter. His right hand and his queen stolen in one swift attack. This was a brazen act of war.

A war for the heart and soul of Meradin. And her beloved

queen.

The End
Book Two

Hello again,

Thank you so much for reading this book. If you enjoyed it, even a little, would you do me a huge favor? Please take a few minutes and write a review, and if you know someone who would enjoy this book, send them a little note and tell them about it.

If you're intimidated by writing a review, here's a blog post I wrote a few years ago to help readers formulate a helpful review: **https://kirstensblacketer.com/2018/01/11/how-to-write-a-helpful-review/**

An honest review is like a love letter to the author. It helps us grow and lets us know our hard work is appreciated. Though it may seem simple and insignificant, it means the world to hear your thoughts. Thank you for taking the time to show your love.

Also, if you'd like to be the first to know when I have a new release or get some sneak peeks into my current WIPs, then sign up for my monthly newsletter. When you subscribe, you'll get a free steamy historical short story. You can only get it as a loyal subscriber to my newsletter. I'll be offering other special short stories and giveaways as well. You won't want to miss it. You can find the sign up form on my website:

https://kirstensblacketer.com

Thank you again for your love and support! I look forward to chatting with you soon.

Sincerely,

Jen Bradlee/Kirsten S. Blacketer

ABOUT THE AUTHOR

Jen Bradlee is the alter ego of author Kirsten S. Blacketer.

Jen Bradlee can get away with murder, metaphorically speaking of course. She enjoys people watching, belly dancing, and taking walks in the rain. Give her a man who isn't afraid to get his hands dirty and plays hard. The ones with rough edges and a little scruff are the best. Comes with a warning label. "Too hot to handle."

Inspired by Tom Hiddleston and Benedict Cumberbatch, she creates characters who have multiple facets to them. The gentleman in the streets but with a wild, dangerous side behind closed doors. She loves villains and anti-heroes, bad boys and irredeemable men. We all have a dark side. Sometimes it must be freed.

http://kirstensblacketer.com/jen-bradlee